DJINN UNLEASHED

The Elven-Trinity Book 1

MARK ALBANY

Mark Albany
Copyrighted Material.

FOREWORD

I hope you enjoy this book. It is strictly for adults, but if you are 18+ and enjoy the read, come join me and two other authors in our Facebook group, HAREM NATION.

We look forward to discussing our books with you!

❧ 1 ❧

A shudder ran down my spine. I knew my imagination made everything so much worse than reality actually was, but in my mind, there wasn't much that could be worse than having spiders running up and down my back. It was probably dust bunnies, I told myself, dropping from the ceiling. I knew for a fact that nobody had been all the way up here with a duster since last winter.

I froze, feeling something tickling its way down my back, under my shirt. Dust bunnies didn't crawl across skin like that. I felt the need to shout and slap until there was nothing but mush where that damn spider was. Thoughts of the different species flashed through my mind. White ghost spiders could kill a man with a bite. A couple of red spiders could leave me with a nasty infection and fever for weeks.

Odd how all that seemed to fade when I realized what would happen to me if I was caught up here. Death or fever were nothing compared to what would happen if Master Vis found me sneaking around in the rafters of the manor.

All of it was enough to make me wonder just what the fuck I was doing up here in the first place. What did I stand to gain, even if I wasn't caught?

I was looking for something to help me in my training, but if I was discovered, it would all have been for nothing.

I lowered myself from the rafters, careful to slow my descent so as not to be heard. My soft shoes made barely a whisper over the flagstones. I quickly pushed my hand down over the area where there was still something tickling my back, breathing a sigh of relief when I realized it was just a trickle of sweat.

I stepped lightly, keeping my center of gravity low to the ground as I moved closer to the door. I could hear voices inside. I should have been more afraid than I was, but at this point, I was more afraid of what would happen if I didn't do this.

Evening rituals were rare. Well, not so much rare as difficult to find. There was a good deal of taboo that still surrounded magic, thanks to the history of abuse, but that very history was what made it so very popular with the few who could withstand the public scorn if they practiced it.

I gritted my teeth, freezing in place when I heard the sound of heavy boots outside. Master Vis' manor, where I resided, wasn't that far away from the guard-house that provided security not only for the capital, Ozryn, but for the rest of the empire as well. Discovery here would end poorly for me.

I need to be more cautious, I thought, crouching as I moved closer. My soft, calfskin shoes made little noise over the stones. My breathing was the loudest noise to be heard until I got closer to the open arch, which led to Master Vis' chambers. I pressed against the marble walls, making myself as invisible as possible before peeking around the corner.

Master Vis was there, dressed in black and red silk. Odd, all things considered. He hated flowing robes. He always said they made him look fat. Considering that the man always looked painfully thin, I had no idea what he was even talking about, but there were certain vanities that could not be judged from man to man.

My eyes immediately flickered over to the two women with him. Both had the look of ladies of note, judging from the way that their long, red locks were styled, elegantly brushed and held up by silver and gold wire. That and the paint on their faces were all I had to go on, as they were otherwise naked. Full, heavy breasts, toned stomachs and supple legs were all I could see as they moved around Master Vis. I couldn't hear what they were saying as they whispered in his ear, but the intonation was clear, as well as the man's reaction.

He grinned, the small, fine wrinkles around his mouth disappearing as he leaned in and kissed one woman's neck gently. She giggled, mock-slapping his face as the other woman grinned, moving over to the bed in the center of the room. The first woman joined her as Vis moved over to them. I couldn't imagine that this was how rituals were conducted. There had been images in my mind of pasty old men in long robes chanting ominously. I couldn't have imagined something further from the truth.

Vis stood over the women, who lay prone on their backs. His hands moved over them, a foot or so above their naked bodies as he started chanting something in a deep, almost unnatural voice. I'd heard him speak that way before. He was a spellcaster, whose power lay in the spoken word. The man had more than a few books devoted to the craft. I'd always been interested, but as a familiar, it had never been my place to learn more than the rudimentary details. I was a focusing point for Vis' magic.

While I was far from the best familiar, I wasn't the only one in Master Vis' employ either. Which begged the question of why the man was choosing not to conduct this ritual with any of his available familiars. I suspected that the answer lay with the women over whom he was performing the incantation. They were nobles, who would have demanded as few witnesses as possible.

As Vis continued his incantations, I could see bright marks starting to show on the women's skin. They started out as bright spots, but slowly started taking the form of runes. I narrowed my eyes, unable to make out what the runes were supposed to represent. Then again, my training in that area had been lacking at best.

I saw an aura starting to build around Vis. What little I did know was that the more power he took into himself, the faster he needed to expend it, lest it start to build up an excess. There were conflicting stories about what happened if the amount of power reached a critical point, since most mages used familiars to transfer the power to if things got too hot.

In this case, quite literally, I realized as the silk robes Vis was wearing started to smoke. The man gritted his teeth as he tried to quickly finish the incantation before his clothing caught on fire.

He didn't have enough time. A sleeve burst into flame. Vis jumped back, shouting a curse as he pulled away. The marks on the women's bodies immediately started to retreat and disappear as the women sat up from their prone positions, looking more disappointed than concerned as Vis rushed out of the room, trying to douse the flames.

He was running in my direction. I had barely a moment to pull away from the arch before he rushed through it, more preoccupied with the burning sleeve than with paying attention to his surroundings.

He stepped into the darkened room I was hiding in, pulling the ruined sleeve off with a growl as he cradled his burned arm. I could see that the flame hadn't done as much damage as I had feared. I suspected that his ego took the brunt of the damage.

"Should have brought a fucking familiar." Vis stared, then whispered a few words of power to cool his arm off.

This was my chance. Distracted as he was, I could make an escape and move away into the shadows.

"Grantham?" I heard him say as I turned away. The sound of his voice was the last thing I wanted to hear, especially saying my name. There was no escaping, no running away.

And from the sound of it, he wasn't too pleased to see me.

"I..." I gasped, trying to work up a response, "I thought you might have needed a... needed a familiar for your ritual?"

"What?" Vis hissed, moving in closer to me. He gripped my shoulder, spinning me around.

"You... you needed a familiar?" I repeated. I had no illusions that my claim would help me escape punishment for snooping, but I couldn't think of anything else to say.

"Were you spying on me?" he asked, putting a hand on my forehead. I closed my eyes, trying to fight back a panicked sob. Vis had ways of getting to the truth of a matter without torture. Well, physical torture anyways. I remembered the day he had demonstrated that to the rest of the familiars, using me as example.

It had felt like a thousand needles digging into my skull. I closed my eyes, shaking my head. "I would never spy on you!" I cried softly. "I swear."

He pushed me to my knees, leaving his hand on my temple. I wasn't sure if he had already started the spell or not, but he quickly pulled his hand away, chuckling.

"No, I don't believe you would," Vis said, shaking his head. "Even so, you should not have been here. Come with me, and we shall decide on a punishment for your actions."

* * *

I LOOKED AROUND THE DARK CELLAR, WHICH WAS lit with only a couple of candles. The dank room had walls made of rough rock.

"I was not spying on you, Master Vis," I whispered again, once he finished putting a listening ward on the door and turned back to me.

"I believe you," Vis said softly, inspecting his burnt arm.

"Then, what...?" I couldn't shake the feeling of terror that was starting to soak through me.

"I will not punish you, boy," Vis said, smiling and patting my cheek gently. I was a good foot taller than he was, and yet I still felt like he towered over me the same way he had when I was a child.

"Why?" I asked, not believing my good luck and unable to keep from voicing the first thought that came to mind.

"Because I have a job for you," Vis said softly. "It will be risky, but I believe you can handle it. While your skills in my craft are lacking, I know you have what it takes to see this task to completion. It will be different from what you have been taught your whole life, but I believe that to be a boon rather than a curse in this instance. Get it done, and we'll both reap the benefits."

I nodded. While in the immediate future, this was better than spending the night having Vis practice his spells on me, I couldn't imagine that whatever this task was would be easy. It wasn't like I had much of a choice, though.

I ground my teeth and nodded. Vis had many ambitions, most of which he wasn't very likely to achieve considering his low rank even among the nobility, but if there was one thing I knew, there wasn't much that Vis wouldn't do to advance those positions.

The only problem was, it seemed like now I would be the one doing those things instead.

❧ 2 ❧

I'd been asked to steal for Vis before. The man had little in the way of scruples and seemed more than happy to encourage his low morals in those under his command. I had average looks and a build that made me more or less invisible anywhere but the Slums, and that, added to my lack of natural ability, made me the best choice for doing Vis' dirty work.

No, that wasn't fair, I thought as I made my way toward the palace. When my parents died, Vis had been the one to take me in, teach and feed me, and put a roof over my head. If it hadn't been for him, I would have ended up in the Slums, which as things were at the moment, were by far the worse option. I could do a little stealing and tolerate a little abuse if it meant staying away from the areas of the city cordoned off for the poorest of the poor.

Then again, I was breaking into a noble's house this time. Nobles had connections to mages much more powerful than Master Vis, and if the man himself was any indication, getting caught would result in a fate much worse than anything I would find in the manor I called home.

"Just... don't get caught," Vis had said as he laid out his plans. We'd looked them over by candlelight in that dark, dank cellar.

He had put together a surprising amount of intelligence on the house he wanted me to break into. I wasn't sure why I was surprised. Vis was no moron, and certainly knew how to do his research. Even so, I wasn't sure if these plans and details had come from him. It all seemed rushed since less than an hour after being caught, I was ushered off the manor's premises with the hope that I had memorized everything I needed to know before heading out.

Vis had seemed flustered. I'd never seen him like that. Even among other nobles, he had always seemed witty, calm, and in control. Whether it was because of his failed ritual before or something else entirely, something had my master on edge, and I wasn't sure what to make of it.

I brought my mind back to the present. I had always made a point of memorizing the movements of the guards in the area. Mostly just to pass the time, but also a useful mental exercise, as I had grown used to Vis using me for this kind of work. Knowing when the men in red and gold uniforms were making their rounds was probably why I had survived this long.

Small things always added up to big figures, I remembered reading somewhere. Had it been in the 'Tale of the Sisters Three'? It was possible. Too much time had passed since I had been allowed free rein of the manor's library. Ever since I had tried to sneak into the section that contained the books on words of power, I wasn't allowed in there without a chaperone.

I took a deep breath, pausing behind a pillar as I counted down the seconds until the guards' next pass. These weren't the kind that patrolled the lesser areas of the city. Even the houses of the nobles were protected by the Emperor's Lancers, men of high training and discipline. They wouldn't dawdle or distract themselves with conversation. It made sneaking around them difficult, but it also meant that they made their rounds at the same time each and every night, without fail.

Right on time, two men moved around the corner of the house. Their armor gleamed like it was cleaned and polished every day, and they marched in time with each other, never a step off beat as they came across the road. I sidled around the column in front of Lord Drake Pollock's manse, keeping to the shadows as they passed, listening as their heavy boots crashed onto the cobbles, moving further and further away.

I pulled a smooth pebble from my pocket once they were far enough away from the entrance that I didn't have to worry about them seeing me as I vaulted over the low wall that encircled Pollock's house. I liked keeping the small rocks I found at the edge of Kaesor's Lake, the smooth, pretty ones. I liked the look and feel of them, especially the way they felt warm even if left outside on a chilly night.

More importantly, though, I liked them for their weight, and how easy they were to aim and throw. It was odd how often that ended up being useful.

I hefted the pebble in my hand, staying low to avoid being seen by the guards who were patrolling the grounds. These would be mercenaries, former soldiers in need of coin and lacking in the discipline of the Lancers, but still formidable for an eighteen-year-old familiar. I needed them distracted and very far away as I made my entrance.

I peeked over the wall. One of the hanging lanterns was close enough for me to hit with my stone, but not so close it would draw their attention to my hiding spot. I drew my hand back and flicked it forward, using my fingers to spin the flat pebble as it arced through the air.

There was a moment of satisfaction as I saw it strike the lantern hard enough to break the ceramic, spilling the oil over the grass on the ground, as well as the still-lit wick.

The fire that resulted hadn't been what I had in mind, but it caused shouting and general pandemonium as the oil-soaked grass caught fire.

Nobody was looking as I smoothly vaulted the low wall, taking care to hide myself in the bushes and crawling over the ground to reach the house itself. Thanks to the fire starting to spread, I had no trouble finding a door left open to slip into the building. My clothes were standard for servants of this area, the bland, grey robes that made sure the people remained invisible to those they served.

I picked up a bucket that was left behind by one of the others and jogged quickly into the manse, following the routes I'd memorized from Vis' papers, which guided me through the maze that was Pollock's house. It was massive, much more luxurious than Vis' manor, and more difficult to navigate, especially as I was masquerading as a servant who was supposed to be helping fight the fire outside.

Sure, starting a fire hadn't been my intention, but it didn't look like it was causing too much damage. It was more of a nuisance to the servants and guards than anything else. I tossed the bucket I had been carrying as a disguise aside as I found the entrance to the basement.

Vis hadn't specified what this parchment I was

supposed to steal even did. It was an artifact of magical importance, but more than just something to be looked at and admired. It was an item of power, that much was sure. I was certain that Vis would make sure to keep me out of the loop once the item was retrieved.

Should I make it back alive, that was.

The house was fairly deserted, and not only because of the fire. I had attended a couple of parties at this house with Vis, and it had always been humming with activity. It appeared that Vis' intelligence that Pollock and his wife were currently staying in a house nearer the coast had been correct.

It was odd that Pollock had a magical item in his possession at all. The topic itself was taboo, with most items being held by mages and men of power, and there had been no indication that Pollock was one of those. He was the son of a merchant who had done well enough for himself to purchase a place in the gentry, with the Emperor's records being altered to show him as the descendant of some extinct house.

It was all too far above me to really give a shit about it, but it did raise the question of why there would be something of magical importance within the man's walls.

The shouting faded almost completely as I made my way down the steps that led into the manse's basement. I kept my eyes and ears tuned for the smallest sound or slightest movement. Sure, intelligence was all well and good, but the house being this abandoned, especially this close to something that was supposed to be incredibly valuable, was making me nervous. There had to be defenses set up around the house to keep me from doing precisely what I had just done.

Nobody expected their house to get robbed, which was kind of the point. Even so, I couldn't shake the feeling that things had been going just a little too well. Something was bound to go wrong. As I navigated the expansive maze that made up even the basement I felt myself grow more and more nervous.

Vis would kill to have a manse like this, I realized with a small smirk as I slipped inside the chamber that was supposedly where I would find the piece of parchment.

Again, the absence of any guards at all made me uneasy. The door was locked, but only by a bolt kept in place by a heavy but simple pin tumbler padlock. I pulled out the lockpicks I'd brought with me, dropping to a crouch. The lighting wasn't the best, but these things were best done by feel anyway. Less than a minute later, the padlock popped open.

A three-tumbler padlock. It was like they *wanted* someone to break in.

There were no torches or lamps inside, but those outside the room gave me enough light to find my way inside. There was a pedestal in the center of the room where a simple page of parchment lay.

There was a feeling in my gut telling me to get out. This wasn't worth it. Something was going to go wrong, and I would end up in some dungeon being tortured for information. I could probably make a break for it. The forest was just outside this property. Sure, I didn't know anything about scavenging, hunting, or anything involving survival beyond the comforts of the city, but it had to be better than whatever I had to face in here, right?

Wrong. I shook my head before heading the room, looking around before picking the parchment up.

It resisted my tug, almost like there was an invisible force around it keeping my fingers from reaching it while keeping it on the pedestal.

It had little strength, but the moment I lifted the piece, a soft gong sounded somewhere. Not in this room, but close by. In the basement.

"Fuck!" That was all I had time to say before I heard boots stomping. They had to have been nearby to react this quickly, and the gong that had alerted them to my presence made them move a lot quicker than anticipated.

It wasn't long before there was a pair of men in

full plate armor in front of me, each carrying a club in one hand and a torch in the other.

"Who the fuck are you?" one of the men asked, coming in closer.

"I'm... here to make sure the parchment is kept safe from the fire outside," I said quickly, not sure where the lie had come from. It wasn't very good.

"That's what we're here for, dumbass," the man on the left said as he approached me. "Put it back and come with us."

"I... cannot stray from my duties, sir," I said quickly, watching as they both started closing in. An idea was starting to form. I knew my way back up to the ground floor, and it would be a simple thing to get out over the wall and to the forest where I could lose all pursuers. All I needed to do was get out of this damned trap of a room.

The man on the right reached me before his comrade, nudging at me with his club. "Wait until Kruger gets his hands on you, worm." He reached down to hook the club into his belt, presumably so he would have a hand free to grab and restrain me without putting his torch down.

I jumped into action almost without thinking. I wasn't much of a fighter, but then again, I wasn't trying to fight. I needed to get away, and that came a lot easier than actually having to beat these men myself. I reached out, grabbing at the man's torch and shoving it into his comrade's face. The man screamed and stumbled back, dropping his torch and club to bat out the fire that had caught on his beard.

Using the distraction, I pushed the first man into the wall behind him and vaulted the pedestal, sprinting toward the door, which I closed and bolted as soon as I passed through. There had been no access to the bolt from the inside, I noted, and that would keep my two friends occupied for the time it took me to escape the grounds.

I could hear shouting as soon as I reached the stairs leading up from the basement, and it told me that my presence had been discovered. It appeared that the gong that had alerted the two to my presence had done the same with the rest of the guard. A few were still working to contain the flames, but there were guards starting to rush toward me.

I still had time. The manse was a maze, which was as much a disadvantage to them as it was to me. I circled around, away from them and in the opposite direction that I'd originally come in, and away from the other men making their way toward me.

I slipped out through one of the doors that had been left open. I could see the forest looming large just over the small, easily-cleared wall. The dark trees were usually daunting, but right now they were a sight for sore eyes as I rushed through the bushes and over the paths, making my way toward the wall. Just a few feet away, I jumped, diving over the wall toward freedom.

The hand carrying the parchment crashed into something just before it reached the perimeter. I felt my whole body pushed back into the garden I was trying to escape. The blow knocked the breath out of me as I blinked, looking at the wall, trying to figure out just what it was that had stopped me from escaping.

I pushed myself back to my feet, hearing the voices from inside the house coming closer. My shoulder and arm were both hurting, but I shrugged the pain off for the moment, reaching for the wall once more.

And once more, my hand crashed into something, bruising my knuckles painfully.

"Fuck!" I cursed, pushing my hand harder against the invisible barrier. There was a bit of give to it. I heard the door that I'd used to leave the house open, and heard shouting as the men that came out saw me.

"Over there!" one of them called. "Tell Kruger to send more men!"

Kruger. I'd heard the name before, in the basement. These men's captain, maybe? I shook my head, growling as the barrier continued to give, but too slowly.

I could hear their boots trampling the bushes and getting closer to me as, suddenly, the barrier gave.

I gasped for breath just in time to land hard on top of the wall, feeling a jolt of pain as my ribs hit the edge.

No time to stop, though. No time.

"Fuck!" I hissed again, pushing myself over the wall. A hand caught hold of my ankle just as I was about to pull away and I landed heavily on the other side.

My other foot lashed out, hammering into the jaw of the man that had grabbed me, hard enough to send him stumbling back, and forcing him to let me go.

I dropped to the ground outside the wall in a pile, wincing as the aches and pains all got worse.

Still no time!

I pushed myself to my feet again, not even bothering to look back this time as I started running toward the forest. If I could just make it to the tree line, I would be safe. Safer, anyway.

Shadows closed around me as the trees blocked out the waning moonlight. I didn't stop, not even then. The voices were still behind me, and I didn't think the barrier would stop them from following me.

No, that seemed to be in place just to stop anyone carrying the damned piece of parchment. I took a deep breath, feeling my legs burning. I still couldn't stop. Not yet.

🎴 3 🎴

I winced, ducking to avoid the branches that were whipping at my face. I touched my skin, feeling a light touch of blood coming from a cut on my cheek, but I couldn't stop now. I could hear shouting from behind me. It was muted, but only because the sounds of my heavy breathing and pounding heart were filling my ears instead. They couldn't be too far behind.

I felt something stick to my face as I avoided another branch. As I tugged at it, I realized that it was a web.

"Fucking spiders," I muttered under my breath as I suddenly felt the need to make sure that there weren't any of the eight-legged freaks crawling around on my body or hidden in my clothes. I shuddered but kept on running.

The worst a spider could do was bite me. I might die, but a few agonizing hours or days of death by spider bite was still better than what would happen to me if I was caught after stealing the parchment. The Lancers would be involved. There were tales of their dungeons, and in some cases, there were rumors of the Emperor's personal magi getting involved in squeezing information out of people like me, to make them give up those who had ordered their actions.

I didn't want to give Master Vis up. I owed the man everything. Unfortunately, the only other option would be to die on the table after days and days of torment.

Those were my only options should I get caught. There was a third option, of course, and it was what I was working toward so hard, pushing deeper and deeper into the damned forest, feeling my legs burning and heart trying to beat its way out from inside my rib cage.

I flicked at my face again, feeling more spider webs getting caught on it, and in the process, lost sight of where I was going. My foot caught on a jutting root and I stumbled a few steps forward before catching myself on the trunk of another tree. At that moment, I saw that the moonlight was shining through unimpeded in front of me, and the tree had kept me from plunging headfirst down a small cliff. *Well, not quite a cliff,* I thought. The slope was gentler and seemed to be covered in rocks and overturned earth, like it was a recent landslide.

I gasped, feeling a sensation of vertigo filling my body as I gripped the tree harder. This was all so fucking crazy. And all because I couldn't contain myself and had to see how a ritual was performed. There was an anecdote involving curiosity and cats, but the exact wording of it escaped me as I looked down at the drop. In the darkness, I couldn't see how far it went.

I turned around, hearing the shouting getting closer, this time joined by the sound of dogs barking in the distance. I gritted my teeth at the thought. I actually loved dogs, but the feeling wasn't going to be mutual in this case. I gritted my teeth, looking at the ground ahead of me and taking a deep breath.

The drop wasn't sharp. There was an incline where a man could slide down if he was lucky. If he was unlucky, he would get caught on a rock, get his legs torn up, and get sent tumbling head over heels.

The chances weren't great, but as of right now, they were better than my chances of survival if I didn't.

"Shit," I growled, still gasping for breath as I took a step back and spared a few seconds to gather my courage, gently tucking the stolen parchment into my pouch before I cleared the edge and started falling. I turned on my side, feeling the loose rocks and soil starting to tear at my pants, leaving scratches all the way up my thighs. I clenched my teeth as I tried to keep myself from falling too quickly.

I succeeded—partially, anyway—and when I reached the bottom there was a gentle shock of impact as I rolled for a few feet before being stopped more harshly by what felt like a wall.

For a moment, it was all I could do just to stay conscious. My whole body hurt, with scratches running up and down my legs and arms. My clothes were mostly shredded, and while it was too dark to see, I could feel blood trickling down from the light cuts that I'd sustained.

Still, it was better than what would have been waiting for me if I hadn't jumped.

I listened as hard as I could, but I couldn't hear any shouting or dogs barking, so I was safe for the moment. Looking around didn't reveal anything. Wherever I was, it appeared to be underground since there was no light from the moon or stars. I reached into the pouch that was thankfully still attached to my waist and grabbed the candle I usually brought along for jobs like this—you never knew when you were going to be skulking around somewhere dark and in need of light, after all—and some striking flint and steel. It took a few tries, as my hands were still shaking, but I eventually got the wick to light. I looked around.

This wasn't a naturally-formed cave. It was the first thought that entered my mind. Stones had been cut and fitted into the walls. The lack of mortar between them spoke of exquisite design. Or would have, if I knew anything about masonry. I'd only read somewhere that stonework that didn't need mortar was the best kind, but had no idea why.

There had been rumors about old buildings buried deep inside this forest, I remembered as I started making my way through the maze that was the ruins. Ancient fortifications against some legendary evil. It was a vast, expansive area, densely covered in trees, which explained why it was only a rumor, but who would have thought that they were this close? And underground, apparently?

I winced, feeling hot wax starting to drip down and coat my fingers, but the sounds of shouting coming from where I had entered the ruins brought my attention back to what it was that I was supposed to be doing. Which was escaping. It would be a maze for them too, I realized, but my chances of escaping would be best if I could get deeper inside the... tunnels? They looked like they could have been buildings once, with time and nature conspiring to cover them up over the years.

How many years had they been hidden like this? And how much longer would they have remained undiscovered if there hadn't been a landslide?

I shook my head. I had just learned a lesson about how deadly curiosity could be. I didn't want to learn it a second time. I gripped the candle tighter, moving carefully so as not to lose more wax, and moved deeper into the tunnels. They seemed to stretch on forever, but even as I was moving deeper, I could hear shouts coming from behind me. They'd left the dogs behind, it seemed, and were coming in personally to find me. An unexpected boon, I realized, taking a left when the path diverged.

A few minutes later, and a few random choices to keep the men who were after me guessing at my current location, the heat of the chase was starting to fade. I could feel the adrenaline in my body seep away, and all the pains, aches and bruises I'd suffered were starting to make themselves loudly known. My hands were shaking and I could feel exhaustion starting to fill me as I stumbled over the stone ground.

I had to find somewhere to rest. I wasn't going to make it back to Vis' manor tonight, not in the state I was in and certainly not with however many score of mercenaries were between myself and the only exit from this place that I knew about. I needed to find someplace to lay low, lick my wounds, and rest until morning when hopefully some light would filter in. I had taken the paths at random, and I wasn't sure I would be able to find a way out without some help.

I paused, seeing a small room off to the left of the tunnel that I was walking down. Evidence that a door once existed remained in the form of a couple of rusted hinges, but the wood was gone. I slipped inside, careful now as my candle was starting to burn low. I had another one in my pouch, but I didn't want to have to use it just yet. As I moved inside, I immediately regretted it. The walls were lined with coffins, neatly tucked into small cubbies carved out of the solid rock.

My breaths were coming in pants as I looked toward the end of the room, which wasn't even that large. One of the coffins had been disturbed. It was located in a place of honor on a pedestal, removed from the walls that held the others. Unlike the rest, which were untouched and heavy with dust, this one's lid was laying half off. I moved closer, expecting to find a selection of bleached bones or a pile of human remains, but instead, what I found was a good deal more disturbing.

A woman, a noble by her clothes, was lying inside, eyes closed like she was sleeping. There was some discoloration to her skin, indicating that she was, in fact, dead. I reached out to gently nudge her cheek with my forefinger, feeling clammy skin and resistance to my touch that indicated that she had been dead for a while, yet not long enough to start smelling of rot or decay.

Now that I thought about it, this place, though it had been deserted for so long, somehow didn't smell of destruction. There had been no sign of fighting, no scorch marks on the walls. It was like people had just suddenly decided to leave.

Until this woman had shown up, I realized, pushing the lid off completely. The wood dropped to the ground with a loud *crack*, immediately shattering into several pieces.

"Shit," I hissed, telling myself to quiet down as I looked over the rest of her, using my candle for light. There wasn't much else. Her clothes still looked fresh, untouched by the dust that had settled on everything else. No sign of injury, no wound or bruises, or anything like that. It was like she had just come here, laid down in a coffin, and died.

Odd. I caught a glimmer out of the corner of my eye, seeing a small ring on the woman's hand. I was no grave robber, and yet there was something about it that grabbed my attention. I wasn't sure what it was, but before I realized what I was doing, I was tugging at the ring. It came off her finger easily and was quickly curled into the palm of my hand.

Maybe I *was* a grave robber.

I heard the sound of bowstrings being loosed just in time to duck as a crossbow bolt sped a scant inch over my head, burying itself in one of the coffins and causing a cloud of dust to puff up.

There was no time to think about the fact that the dust was actually human remains as I quickly sped around the pedestal, dropping my nearly-spent candle and leaving it behind to sputter out on the ground. There were enough torches lit at the entrance to let me see just how fucked I was.

"Shit," I hissed again. How had they found me? More importantly, how had they managed to sneak up on me like that? It wasn't like I hadn't been paying attention.

"Give up now, thief!" a man shouted from the entrance of the room. I wondered why they weren't rushing in and realized that they thought I was probably armed.

Vis had sent me away without any weapons. I didn't blame him, and yet now that I was staring at a group of angry mercenaries, I wondered if it was the smart choice. It wasn't like I would be able to fight my way through them, yet a dagger might be put to better use by slashing my own throat and not giving these men the opportunity to question me.

It was a moot point right now, but something to remember for future robberies, should I survive this one.

I could hear footsteps moving over the ground. The mercenaries had apparently decided that they weren't going to wait for me to give up. I quickly tucked the ring into my pocket a second before they came around.

I tugged the parchment out of my pocket. I didn't have any weapons, but there might be some use I could get from the object I had stolen. There was writing on it, but for the life of me, I couldn't understand any of it. Odd letters and symbols that I'd never seen before covered the page. There was something about them that tugged at my memory. Maybe I'd seen this kind of writing before? I looked down as I thought I felt the ring in my pocket vibrate, but was interrupted when the mercenaries came around the sarcophagus.

They weren't happy about the merry chase I'd taken them on, if their roughness was any indicator. I was dragged to my feet. I felt a fist hammer into my gut, knocking what little breath I had left out in a gasp. By the time I was able to breathe again, they had started dragging me away.

Torches. Why hadn't I thought to bring a torch instead of a fucking candle?

They took my pouch away, ripping it off of my waist as they pulled me down the hallway. They seemed to know their way around these tunnels, I realized, as it wasn't long before I could see moonlight shining over the ground. Apparently, by jumping down the landslide, I had taken the more difficult route. There was a proper entrance, though it too was overgrown by weeds and bushes, with trees hanging heavily over the stone arches. There were a couple more men waiting outside. They looked like they wanted a try at knocking the breath out of me as well, but the man who was apparently their captain waved them off.

"The boy has a good deal of suffering already in his future." The man, assumedly Kruger, pushed me to the ground roughly. "He'll be turned over to the Emperor for questioning. The Lancers are on their way to collect him now."

"What?" the man asked, nudging my shoulder with his boot, knocking me back down as I tried to regain my feet. "What does the Emperor have to do with a simple burglary gone wrong?"

"No fucking clue," Kruger said. "All I know is, the moment he left the premises, Lancers showed up, demanding him. Now bind him the fuck up and have him ready to hand over to the pricks in armor when they get here. I'm going back in to try and find the rest of the cunts who are in there."

"It's a maze," the first man said with a chuckle. "How are you going to find them all in time?"

"Shut up and bind him," I heard Kruger say as he walked in the way we'd come out. The man still standing over me mumbled a curse, pulling some rope from his belt. He pulled me up into a seated position before binding my hands in front of me.

"So," the man grumbled, pushing me to sit back against the arch. "What the fuck did you steal that caused the Lancers to be jumping to throw you into the dungeons, eh?"

I rolled my eyes. There were a couple of dead vines circling around the archway that were digging into my back. It was uncomfortable, but then again, everything was uncomfortable at this point.

"Fine," the man snarled, taking my chin in his hand and tilting my face up to look at him. "Don't say nothing. Keep your trap shut. I'm sure the fuckers in the dungeon like pretty boys like you. Well, not so pretty anymore, are we?" He prodded a couple of cuts and bruises I'd collected on my face during my attempt at escape.

I gritted my teeth. Whether the dungeons were actually as bad as the rumors made them out to be, I wasn't sure. I knew that fear of the unknown usually ended up being worse than what the reality was, especially for people like me with a vast imagination. Then again, the imagination of those gifted with magical abilities tended to be similarly vast, and they had a lot more experience than I did.

I took a deep breath, trying to calm myself. The mercenary standing over me smirked and patted my cheek.

"I almost feel sorry for you," he said with a

chuckle. "Almost. You made me run after you. And I hate running."

He turned away, chuckling softly. *It was nice that he was able to amuse himself,* I thought, tugging gently at my restraints. The ropes were thin, but still strong enough that breaking free would require a sharp instrument, which I was sadly lacking.

I looked up when I heard heavy boots crunching dead leaves and gravel. I knew that sound. I'd spent whole days memorizing it. Three men in shiny armor that gleamed in the moonlight stepped into view. With them was a shorter man with a hooked nose and balding head who looked terrified of being out here in the night.

"Where's Kruger?" the smaller man asked in a nasal voice.

"He's still in there," the guard said, nodding back toward the tunnels. "We sent a few teams of our boys in there and they're having some difficulty finding their way back out."

The man shook his head, muttering a couple words and waving his hand over the arch as he moved closer to me. I saw the telltale inscription of runes appearing on the stones. This man was a mage.

What the hell had I tried to steal?

"What's this one?" the mage asked, looking down at me, narrowing his eyes.

"Just a boy," the guard said with a smirk. "He's the

one we found with the parchment, though he would have needed help to get past the barrier you put in place. We're searching for them now. They must be in there, too."

"You need to find them quickly," the mage said, pulling his robes around himself with bony fingers. "I don't like being out here at this time. There are foul omens in the air."

"Whatever you say," the guard said with a chuckle. Even among mages, omen-readings were generally discarded as fiction and snake-oil peddling. The mage scowled venomously at the man.

"I'm going inside to find Kruger," he said after a moment. "You lot," he indicated the three Lancers, "keep watch on the boy. We'll take him back when we return. Put him in some dark hole to think about the error of his ways."

I sighed, leaning back against the arch, watching the mage disappear. Well, at least the torture wouldn't be starting just yet. I rubbed idly at the wax that had collected on my fingers until I remembered the ring in my pocket. They hadn't searched me yet, taking only my pouch, but they were bound to eventually, and they would find it if it remained where it was.

I moved slowly, avoiding attention as I slipped my fingers into the pocket of my pants, finding the small, round circlet. It was hard to tell by touch, but I thought that there had been a gem studded into the top of the ring. I rubbed my fingers over the smooth metal. It was warm to the touch—not surprising considering that it had been in my pocket, pressed close to my skin—but I couldn't find any gem. I rubbed my finger over it again, trying to check, tilting my head. Fucking thing was messing with my mind—

"What do you desire?"

I heard the voice right next to my ear, so close that I could feel hot breath on my cheek. I started, falling to the side away from the voice, looking up to see where it had come from. The Lancers didn't seem to notice my movements, or if they did, they didn't care. The guard had moved off while I'd been distracted. I couldn't see him. What I could see was a woman.

No, not a woman, I realized as she moved out of the shadows. There were tattered wings jutting from her back, and curled, black horns on the crown of her head. Her skin was dark, though exactly what color it was proved difficult to tell in the poor lighting. I could see that her hair was green, though, and that her eyes almost seemed to be glowing, or at least reflecting what little light there was around us, and that she was wearing... next to nothing. Skimpy pieces of clothes that gleamed like metal and yet moved like silk covered her body, but only just, leaving a distracting amount of bare skin to view.

It was odd to find something so different so attractive.

She smiled, leaning closer to me again. "Want I should get rid of them?" she asked with a tilt of the head toward my bindings. I wasn't sure how she could, or why. I was thoroughly confused, but her question was the one thing I had an answer to at the moment.

I nodded.

She nodded, pulling a knife from... thin air, it appeared, and easily slashed through them before turning away. I moved quickly, not sure where this woman had come from, why she was helping or what I was going to do once my luck ran out—but there was one thing I had come here for, and I wasn't leaving it behind. I quickly crawled over to my satchel, which was placed next to the parchment that I'd stolen, and looked around.

The Lancers looked like they had at least tried to put up a fight but hadn't been able to. Roots had grown up from the ground around them, wrapping around their legs, pinning them in place. I could see that the roots had also slipped underneath their armor, and from the looks in their eyes through their helmets, I could tell that what the roots were doing was less than comfortable.

I turned to see the woman... thing, walking toward me. The runes left on the archway were glowing again, but this time they seemed to be dissipating, one by one.

"We cannot stay," she whispered, coming closer and kneeling next to me. I opened my mouth to give voice to the hundreds of questions that were coming to mind, but she didn't give me time to speak. She placed her hands on my temples and closed her eyes. I only had a moment to realize that her horns had started to glow before the world around me started to twist and disappear. I felt nausea starting to rise from my stomach as everything went black, and yet continued to twist somehow, and we were suddenly moving. I couldn't tell if it was forward or backward, but we were moving. Somewhere.

❧ 4 ❧

We stopped so suddenly that my head snapped forward, just barely avoiding a collision with her chest before I pulled myself back up, looking into her eyes again. They weren't glowing. And neither were her horns, not anymore. I opened my mouth, but nothing came out for the longest of moments. The blackness and twisting were gone, but the nausea remained. There was also a powerful, pounding ache in my head and I felt myself heaving, trying to keep the contents of my stomach in place.

When I managed to recover my composure, I realized that we were back at Vis' manor. Not only that, but we were in my room, and I was sitting on the tiny little cot that had been my bed for the past decade or so.

And the woman-thing was kneeling in front of

me, a smug if slightly mutinous look on her face as she peered up at me, like she was expecting me to say something.

I needed to say something.

"What... Who... are you?" I asked, hoping she wouldn't take offense that one or the other word was wrong.

"My name is Aliana," she answered, looking like the name was supposed to answer all the other questions that were coming. It didn't.

"Name... my name is Grantham," I said, not wanting to be impolite to the woman who had potentially just saved my life. "But, er, I go by Grant."

She stared at me, unblinking, then said. "That's a ridiculous name." Her voice was soft, flowing, like music that conveyed the mood she seemed to be in. It was curious and enjoyable.

"What are you?" Maybe I meant to ask who she was or for her name, but the words were out before I could think.

"I am one of the Sisters Three, bound to that ugly little ring that is nestled in your pocket," she said.

I paused, taking a moment to think about it. I recognized something about what she had said, and from more than just the books I'd been reading.

"Sisters Three?" I asked, tilting my head. "You're a djinn? Stuck in this ring?"

"So, you do know what I am," she said, sounding pleased.

"Well, yes, who doesn't?" I asked. "The Sisters Three is a nursery rhyme meant to teach children about the dangers of excessive greed. You came when I needed you, but... only once I had the ring?" Things were starting to make sense. There had been books and scrolls studying the possible existence of djinn beyond children's fairy tales, but the conclusion that had been drawn was that, if they did exist, the implications would make things a whole lot more complicated than the simple granting of wishes.

The scroll had somehow guided me to the tunnels, to the sarcophagus where the ring had been, and when I'd looked into it, nudged me toward using the ring. I'd fucked it up the first time around, but was given the chance to try again, and had accidentally taken advantage.

Master Vis was right. I did suck at magic.

I heard footsteps coming up the stairs to where my room was. I looked around, realizing that if there was someone coming, I would have a lot to explain without having a near-naked djinn in the room with me.

"Hide now, quickly," I said urgently. She smiled indulgently and in the blink of an eye, she was gone again, disappearing as quickly as she had appeared in the first place. I tugged the ring out of my pocket, feeling that it was a lot hotter than it had been before, and hid it under the straw mattress of my cot before the door opened.

As the door opened, creaking loudly, it was all I could do not to wince and cover my ears. For some reason, however it was that Aliana had brought us here had left me with a pounding headache.

As surprised as I was to find Vis coming to my quarters himself, it was no match for how surprised he was when he saw me.

"Fuck!" he shouted, dropping the candle that he'd brought with him for light.

"Master Vis?" I asked, standing up quickly from my bed, trying to ignore the ring I'd left behind.

"Grantham?" Vis asked, tilting his head as he reached down to collect the candleholder that he'd let fall in his surprise. "How did you get here? I'd heard... I'd heard they caught a thief breaking into Lord Pollock's manse and assumed the worst."

His words were supposed to be comforting, but the way he narrowed his eyes and stared at me made me wonder if he wouldn't have some suspicions about my story. I steeled my nerves, putting my mind to work, even if it was in pain.

"You didn't send me out to fail, Master," I said softly, pulling the piece of parchment from my pouch and handing it to him. I could see, even in the dim light of the still-lit candle that Vis' eyes quickly lit up when he saw it. He clearly knew what it was, as he snatched it out of my hands, cradling it in his fingers as if it were a newborn babe. I actually wondered if Vis would treat a newborn with the amount of reverence he was showing to this piece of paper.

"You didn't try to use it, did you?" Vis asked, still staring at the parchment, running his fingers over the faded letters.

"I wouldn't even know how," I answered truthfully, adding a slight shrug. "I don't use magic. You are aware of this."

Vis looked up at me. I could see something like fear in his eyes, coupled with suspicion as he took a few steps closer to me. I could smell the wine on his breath as he leaned in. I knew he was considering whether or not he needed to put me to the test to see if I was telling the truth. I tried not to squirm at the thought, and only partially because of the uncomfortable nature of the test.

After what felt like years, Vis took a step back, a fake smile playing on his lips, his hand patting me on the head instead of pressing to my temple. "You did well. Very well indeed. I'll be honest, I actually thought this task would be beyond what even you would be able to perform. That said, it would be best if we both laid low for the time being. If my part in this scheme were to come to light, there is no telling what the consequences will be, and his Lordship will definitely be looking for someone to blame for this piece of parchment slipping through his fingers. Get some rest and... treat your wounds." He said that while looking at the bruises and cuts on my body like I was a leper before quickly turning and walking out of my room. "I'll send some food up for you."

I nodded, wincing again as the door slammed. My head was still pounding when one of the manor servants came in with a tray of soup with bread and a jug of clear, cool water from the well outside, as well as a cloth and a bowl full of water to wash myself with. I ate like I'd been starved, leaving the tray outside my door before taking the cloth and quickly washing away the dried blood that had collected on my face and body. My clothes were ruined beyond repair.

I tossed the dirty, ruined clothes to the side as I pulled on a fresh set. They were of the same drab grey color, but at least they were clean and had not been put through the hellish gauntlet of running through a forest and falling down a landslide.

Even between that and how late it was, I wasn't able to bring myself to sleep yet. There were only a couple of hours until sunrise, and in spite of the annoying, plaguing exhaustion that was slipping into my body, as the lights went out and I lay back in my bed, I found my mind going back to the ring I'd picked up and the woman who seemed bound to it.

A djinn. I wasn't even sure if I believed it. I thought about it while pulling the ring out from under the mattress and staring at it closely in the moonlight shining in through the shutters. It was made of bronze, with a small green gem embedded in the side. It looked cheap and poorly made.

"She's right," I murmured, gently rubbing at the bronze to get it to shine a bit. "It really is an ugly little ring."

"That is what I said," I heard her say, again close enough that I could feel her breath.

I resisted the urge to jump away like I had before, but my heart was hammering and I almost fell off the bed.

"You have to stop doing that," I insisted.

She grinned in response. "And how would you expect me to appear? Through a door, maybe through the window?"

"Well, that wouldn't be the worst thing," I replied. Now that she said so, it did seem a bit silly to expect someone that came into view because of a ring to take a door because it would make me more comfortable.

She moved away from the bed, looking around the room as I tried to keep from gawking. She hadn't improved her dress from nearly naked. Her wings were clearly visible, I realized, and looked like they had been torn at by wild beasts, drawing my attention away from the silky smoothness of her nearly-bare skin.

"I didn't know djinn had wings," I said softly.

She turned toward me, tilting her head as a playful smile teased at her lips. "And just how did you expect djinn to appear, Grant?"

"I'm not really sure," I said, remaining in bed, forcing myself to look away. "There hasn't been anyone who could reliably claim that they had met with one before now, so all visual depictions range from massively unknowable and powerful, to... well, the sort of small, round, inoffensive thing that would appear in the realm of children's stories. Certainly, never something quite as..." I struggled to find the right word.

"Horrifying?" Aliana said helpfully, flicking a strand of hair from her face as she looked at me. "Awe-inspiring? The kind of thing to make any man's blood run cold?"

"Distracting," I corrected her, as I tried not to stare. It was hard not to let my eyes lock onto her barely-contained breasts.

I could see her give that playful smirk I'd begun to associate with her as she turned away, flicking her wings gently as she walked over to the single window of my room. She quickly undid the bolt on the shutters and pulled them open, taking a small breath. Of all the things I had to be thankful for in this tiny room, the biggest was the view it afforded. It was only the second story of the servants living quarters, and yet the ground fell away sharply, giving an amazing view of the small lake that lay just beyond Vis' property and the forest that spread out beyond.

She leaned forward, resting her hands on the windowsill. I smiled, still not having the energy to get out of bed. Besides, it was probably best if I wasn't on my feet or anywhere near her at the moment.

"I wonder what the world is like now," she said softly, looking out at the view.

I shrugged. "How long were you trapped inside the ring? I assume you were trapped, anyway."

She chuckled, and it sounded like music. "I have no idea. It seems like a long time ago, but I think time passes differently while trapped inside that fucking thing. It could have been a hundred years or a thousand, for all I could tell."

"The woman I took the ring from didn't seem to have died that long ago," I said softly, seeing the sadness in her eyes.

"That is to be expected from a magical artifact as powerful as that," she said with a cheerless laugh. "They preserve everything they touch, even if they aren't alive. Even so, it must have been decades at least. My connection to my sisters has faded, and unless they died, it takes years before there is that kind of erosion. Besides, I think that if they were alive, they would have tried to find me by now."

I was about to ask what she was talking about when I remembered how she'd introduced herself. Aliana of the Sisters Three indicated that there were two more sisters.

"Do you miss them? Your sisters, I mean?" I asked, feeling foolish once the words passed my lips.

She smiled, closing the shutters and walking back over to me. "We weren't sisters. Not of blood, anyway. Even so, we were closer than that, somehow. Family of blood cannot be picked, but the family chosen instead of given, gives a much stronger bond, if that makes sense. When I was cursed, I lost that bond. I intend to reclaim it."

I tilted my head. "So, you're telling me that... you haven't always looked this way? You haven't always been a djinn? In all honesty, you do fit the description of a demon more aptly, but then again there aren't many who can claim to have seen any of those either."

She smirked, raising an eyebrow as she joined me on the bed, leaning closer so that there wasn't anything I could do but look at her, and by extension...

"No, I haven't always looked this way," she whispered.

The way her eyes locked with mine, it seemed like

she was trying to attract my attention. Not that she needed to put too much effort into it, I realized, clearing my throat and pulling the light blanket up over my midsection.

"I see," I said, my voice having gone a few tones deeper since the last time I'd spoken. "That's not to say that you don't look... absolutely stunning as you are now. Just very attention-grabbing, is what I mean. I should probably keep my voice down. Others in this building might hear and discover you."

"Unfortunate," she said, pouting adorably. "I do so love making a man scream."

My eyes widened and I could feel heat starting to spread across my cheeks. This was certainly a new experience for me, that was certain, but I wasn't sure what she meant by that. Or rather, I didn't want to make any assumptions about what she meant by it. The reason why magic was such a taboo subject was because it was said that those who wielded it had a tendency toward sadism, and so far, my personal experience had lent itself to that line of thinking. As such, I couldn't tell if she meant screaming in pain or... the other way.

She pulled away, stretching her arms above her head and yawning. Her skin had a soft, silvery glow in the dim light, looking smooth like a peach that I wanted to take, to kiss... My mind filled with images of her on top of me, my hands caressing her curves, removing what little clothing she had, my tongue taking a nipple and twirling around it. Could she possibly know what she was doing to me?

Her eyes moved to me and she pulled her hair back, very aware of my gaze. My reaction was to fake a yawn as well. Even though it wasn't real at first, it become a full-on yawn and I realized how tired I was. Besides, I doubted that Vis would allow me to skip my training just because I had risked my life for something he wanted.

"I should probably get some sleep," I said, burrowing gently into my bed although my eyes were still glued to her. More than anything, I wanted her to tell me it wasn't time for that, that it was time for something far more exciting.

But her playful eyes moved away, and she nodded. "Agreed. If you need me, you know how to call me."

Did I? I opened my mouth to ask her to just confirm my suspicions, but, like she had before, she just seemed to slip out of existence in the blink of an eye, leaving me alone in my dimly-lit room.

I ground my teeth, shuddering gently as I pulled my blanket up over my body and turned over onto my side. Sleep quickly engulfed me in a warm and dreamless rest.

M y right eye peeked open as I felt a stream of light starting to touch it. The shutters in my window didn't latch properly, always opening after a while. A cool morning air and sunlight streamed in.

Memories of the night before came back as I groaned in pain, feeling sore and bruised muscles moving underneath scratched and cut skin, making for a myriad of sensations that made sure I wouldn't be able to get back to sleep, even if I felt like I could lie around for days.

Besides, I knew my presence would be expected at my lessons, despite the fact that Vis had told me to lay low for the moment. More questions would be raised if I wasn't at my lessons as usual, so with a soft curse, I pulled myself up from the bed. I looked down and realized I'd fallen asleep with the ring clutched in my fingers. I turned it around in my fingers, memories of the woman who had come along with it flooding my mind. *The woman who wasn't a woman,* I thought with a chuckle. I thought about how she had mentioned that she hadn't always been a djinn, and how a curse had turned her and her two other sisters into what she was now.

The world was a strange place, I thought to myself as I stood, needing a few seconds to acquire my balance. I walked over to where my dirty, blood-stained clothes were lying in a heap. I needed to turn them in to the seamstress for fixing, and she wouldn't be happy about it. I might as well just toss them in a fire, but then I would only have one set of clothes. There was no telling if Vis would send me out on another trip, after which I might have no clothes.

Grumbling softly, I picked them up and limped out of the room and tucking the ugly ring into my pocket.

I honestly had no idea why Vis insisted on having the tutors teach me magic. They had been trying since I had arrived at this manor, and at no point in over a decade had I ever shown any kind of aptitude for the magic. Familiars needed to have some kind of connection to the magical arts to be of any use to mages, and I had none. Even so, that had never stopped Vis from having me fail these men in stuffy robes and pompous attitudes over and over again.

It had been a while since I'd thought about it, I realized as I lined up with the other familiars going into one of the lessons. I hadn't missed any in the morning, but my waking up late had meant that I didn't get to have any breakfast, as well as having my ears yelled off by the seamstress.

It wasn't like I could blame her. If someone came to me with that mess of destruction and filth, I would have been angry too, especially if there hadn't been a reason given as to why it had happened. Even more so if I was the one who had to clean it. I *should* have been the one to clean them and fix them. That way, I wouldn't have been yelled at—or yelled at less, anyway—and I wouldn't have to go through these annoying motions.

"Take your seats!" our instructor shouted, as we were all dawdling. I was mostly left alone and allowed to move to the back of the classroom, where an apple had been placed on my desk. We'd been given this trick to do ever since we were children. The tutor had told us that it was the starting step for performing greater feats, but since we weren't supposed to be performing greater feats, as that would be left up to those with noble families to make it acceptable, we were forced to perform the same simple trick we'd been performing since we were children. Or in my case, the trick I had failed to perform since I was a child.

It didn't matter. I'd come up with a handful of tricks to help me move the pieces of fruit without actually needing magic. Sure, the tricks had never fooled the tutor before, but it didn't keep me from trying anyway. The better I got at it, the more practice I got at the skills that Vis actually used me for.

Today though, I lacked the energy required to come up with something new and exciting to try.

"Master Porter, sir," I said, raising my hand. "If we can't move the apples, can we eat them?"

A couple of the other youths in the class chuckled. Porter for his part, did not look amused.

"If you failed to reach the dining hall before they closed it for breakfast, that is hardly my concern," he said without looking up from the scroll on his desk. "These apples are meant for training, and training alone. You may not eat them."

I tilted my head. "Are they... magical apples?"

Porter didn't answer, tossing me a glare that made me look down at my table. He shook his head. "Now, as we've discussed. Reach out with your mind, feel the pieces in front of you, and try to move them," Porter said in a voice that showed that he was as bored with this practice as we all were. Even so, I narrowed my eyes, waving my hands over the apple with a flourish. I was tempted to try and eat the apple anyways, since the man would be yelling at me before the class was over whether I did so or not.

For the briefest of seconds, I was tempted to make an honest effort at actually tugging at the apple with my mind. I closed my eyes, trying to reach out into the air around me in the way that almost a dozen previous instructors had tried to get me to do. They had no tips on how to actually achieve the kind of mental balance required. They had all told me that I either had it or I didn't, and this was the kind of skill that could not be taught.

Annoyingly, it seemed they were right. I tried reaching out, but it was like trying to reach up to a ceiling in a dark room while lying down. It was there, it was possible, just not for me.

I sighed, shaking my head. At the back of the class, I could see several of my classmates already taking control of the pieces of fruit in front of them. None were powerful enough to do much with it other than drag it across the table a couple of times, and from the looks of things, it was an exhausting effort.

I made a face that showed how serious I was supposed to be about this and waved my hands over the apple again with a bit of flourish. On one of the waves, I dropped a small piece of thread, tied in a loop over the apple and tugged it back, keeping it hidden under my forearm.

I closed my eyes, leaving one hand over the apple, as if I was trying to reach out with my mind and using a physical gesture to help with the mental process, as my left hand dropped to the table, tugging at the string. It was gentle at first, and I opened my eyes, grinning, watching as the apple moved, just shuddering in place at first, and then starting to move across the table toward me.

I could hear a couple of confused whispers from some of my classmates. I assumed it was the newcomers, who were a few years younger than I was, since the rest had already seen me trying to pull this particular piece of wool over our tutors' eyes.

The apple was almost at the edge of the table when I felt a hand with a massive ring strike me upside my head, making me duck and clutch where I'd been hit.

I looked up to see Porter standing over me with a furious expression on his face. "Fuck."

"Such simple tricks and sleight of hand are not acceptable in this class, Grantham," Porter snapped, adjusting his ring from where it had hit my skull. "Nor will that type of language. Now, apply yourself to your task or leave my classroom immediately."

I nodded. He was clearly a lot more reasonable today than he usually was. I stood to leave as he had instructed, but quickly found his hands settling on my shoulders and pushing me back down.

"Where the hell do you think you're going?" Porter asked, growing angrier with me by the second.

"You just said—" I started but was silenced by another ring-aided slap to the side of my head.

"You will remain seated and perform your task to the best of your ability in silence!" he said, almost shouting, before moving away to inspect the work of my classmates. I kept my head down, my hand coming back up to rub some feeling into where the man's hand had left a sting. This was all just so damned pointless. What the hell was I doing here, anyways? Everyone knew that the only reason I was here was because Vis needed a patsy should his grubby actions of the past come to light, and I didn't need to attend fucking classes for that.

I managed to sneak in a couple of short naps, hiding them behind closing my eyes for concentration and keeping my hand up to pretend that I was still trying. It made the time spent in the room pass by a lot quicker, though I had to be careful to stay awake when Porter came by my table. If it at least looked like I was trying to stay on the task at hand without distracting my fellow students, he mostly left me alone, leaving behind only a couple of frustrated huffs each time he saw that I wasn't making any progress.

I had no idea why he was surprised at this point, but who was I question the great and magical mages?

I left the class feeling more annoyed than I had in a while. I had more than enough cuts and bruises from my adventures the day before, and thanks to Porter, I had a couple more on my head to bring with me to the next class, which was one I normally looked forward to. Hand-to-hand combat techniques were something I could actually use in my horde of tricks. It was something that I actually had some skill at and didn't require any magical ability.

Even so, I was having a hard time moving at all. I really wished I could just retreat to my room and sleep for the rest of the day. Unfortunately, that wasn't going to happen.

A few hours later, I stumbled up the stairs to my room, a handful more bruises on my arms and ribs to show for my efforts. I'd handed out a couple as well, but the fact remained that I was only halfway through the day and already in worse shape than I had been when I started it.

I saw that a tray of food had already been set out for me. I never ate with the rest of the familiars, or even the servants. It was well known that I was something of a pet project for Vis. There had been a couple of whispers that there were other reasons why Vis kept me around, but only a few days had been needed to dispel those rumors. Vis had depraved tastes, but satisfying them was a task left exclusively to women.

And then Vis started to use me as his personal

thief, which was better than his lover, but only slightly.

I sighed, putting the tray on my table and eating slowly. Not because I wasn't hungry, but because one of the larger students had tagged me in the jaw with a bit more strength than necessary during our evasion class. He hadn't landed any other blows, despite spending the entirety of our sparring session attacking.

One hit was all that was needed, though, I thought, rubbing my jaw gingerly.

The day was only halfway done, I realized with a pained chuckle. More classes. More pretending that I was here for something other than just being a low-level thief.

I heard a soft knock on the open door and looked up, seeing one of the house servants peeking in.

"Master Vis would like a word," she said softly, keeping her eyes down. "He says to meet him in the cellar. He says that you know precisely which one."

I nodded. "Thank you, Felicia," I said with a forced smile. She didn't return it, simply backing out of the room again.

I was finished with my meal, and honestly, whatever Vis had in mind for me had to be better than whatever hoops I was going to be jumping through for the rest of the day, so I took a few minutes to rub some feeling into my sore muscles before picking my tray up and heading back out.

The cellar was the same one Vis had dragged me to the night before. It was under the building where he'd taken up residence, which meant that the cellars were in better condition than even the best rooms in the servants' quarters. There were lit torches on the walls, and Vis himself was seated at a table that had lit candles on it as he looked over a couple of scrolls.

"Grantham," he said, looking up and indicating for me to join him at the table, in a chair across from him. "Please, sit. I'm delighted that you could join me."

Vis was well-practiced in honeying his words to make it seem like my presence here had been something I'd chosen to do, and not just something he had ordered me to do. There would have been punishments involved if I had refused, or even showed up late, but sure, he was absolutely delighted that I could be here.

There was a lot to learn from that. I wasn't a noble and wasn't likely to get anywhere in life because someone was handing it to me. I would need to work for it, and sometimes, use honeyed words from a silver tongue if I wanted something without paying too much for it.

I took my seat across from him, keeping my back straight and my eyes down as he continued looking over his papers for a moment. Vis wasn't a particularly large man, although he wasn't too thin, either. There was nothing about his brown hair and eyes, hooked nose and pleasant smile that suggested the cunning mind to be found beneath.

"How are you feeling today?" Vis asked, surprising me enough that I looked up from my lap.

"Just a bit sore from yesterday, Master Vis," I said softly, careful to understate my injuries just a bit. If he wanted a truer tale, all he had to do was look at the bruises and cuts on my face and arms.

Vis smiled. "Yes well, I heard that you weren't quite yourself in the hand-to-hand training and thought it about time we had a little chat."

I looked down again, really hoping he wouldn't grill me on what had happened the day before. I just didn't have it in me to lie about it again. While I wouldn't willingly tell him about the ring in my pocket or about Aliana, if he suspected I was keeping anything from him, all he had to do was apply his magical skills to the task and all would be revealed.

"Grantham," Vis said, making a pyramid with his hands on the table. "I believe it is time for you to learn how to harness the magic that I know to be inside you."

I raised my eyebrows. Of all the topics of conversation, this was certainly not one that I was expecting.

"Pardon me for saying so, master," I said, keeping my tone soft and meek. "But what magic? I've failed every task and lesson that has been placed before me for the past decade."

Vis started at me through narrowed eyes, like he was trying to determine whether I believed what I was saying before responding. The smile that came to his face had the same kind of honeyed quality that his voice had carried before.

"Don't be stupid," Vis said in a condescending manner. "I knew when you were a child that there was magic within you. I have been somewhat... reluctant to make use of it until now, but I am beginning to understand that you might be more useful to me while taking full possession of what you are capable of. Think on what I've said. Take the rest of the afternoon off, get some rest, which you will need, and we shall address the issue in the morning. You may go."

Vis seemed distracted as he was talking, looking down at the papers in front of him with more and more interest until it seemed like he'd almost forgotten that I was there. I shook my head. There was no use in looking the proverbial gift horse in the mouth. If I was getting the rest of the afternoon off from classes, I might as well make the most of it. I took to my feet and quickly exited the cellar before Vis changed his mind and called me back.

In short order, I was back in my room, lying on

my bed. I wanted to take a nice long nap. Vis was right. I needed some rest, no matter what the man had in mind to try and unlock whatever latent magical talent was residing inside me.

And yet, like the night before, I wasn't able to fall asleep. I wasn't sure what Vis had meant when he said there was magic within me, but the fact that he hadn't tried to get it out of me before told me he was probably lying. The reason why wasn't clear, but it had to be something he wanted me to do. Something else he wanted stolen. I really didn't want to think about it, so my mind turned to something else.

I tugged the ring out of my pocket, looking at it closely as I sat up in my bed, throwing my legs over the side. She was beautiful, there was no denying that, and I certainly did want to see her again. But what did that mean? Did I want to see her because of her beauty, or because of her magic?

I was overthinking this. I rubbed gently at the ring's surface, which was how I thought she was supposed to be summoned. She had to hate being stuck in the ring for too long, anyway.

Again, as I looked up, there she was, like she'd just come out of thin air. There was still something about her that just sucked the breath out of me, and not just the oddities like her silver-green hair, or the horns curling up from her head, or even the wings stretching out of her back, though there was some blame laid on the fact that she was wearing practically nothing. Maybe a combination of all those things?

I lost my train of thought suddenly as she moved forward without a word, dropping to her knees, close enough that my attention was immediately brought to where her breasts were almost pressed against my thighs, and her mouth only inches away from where I could feel my blood rushing to. There was no visible reaction yet, but there would be. She seemed like she would make a scene of it, either seriously or in jest, but either way, we had more important things to focus on than my libido.

I reached down, gently taking hold of her arm and pulling her up to sit on the bed next to me.

"What?" she asked, sounding annoyed at being manhandled like that.

"I..." I started, clearing my throat to give me a moment to think about what I could say at this point. "Nothing. I'm just not overly fond of people on their knees in front of me, is all."

She narrowed her eyes, looking at me and seeming to see through the admittedly transparent lie. Even so, she seemed less annoyed and more curious now as she studied me closely.

"I have to say, Grant," she said, her voice soft and soothing. "You are unlike most of the humans I recall."

I opened my mouth, shut it again and nodded. It seemed like a sweeping statement that had a lot of personal observation behind it, yet I wasn't sure where to begin questioning it. I was my own man, of course, but I never thought I was all that different from the rest of my race. Not enough to merit a comment like that, anyway. Sure, there were a lot of people out there who liked having folk on their knees before them, but were there so many that I was the odd person out?

Eventually, I settled on a question I had been meaning to ask since the night before. A bit removed from the current topic of discussion, but that wasn't a bad thing in my mind.

"If you don't mind telling me, how long had you been stuck in that ring before I came along?" I asked, keeping my voice low.

She tilted her head, that smarmy smile touching her bright red lips. "A surprising question, and not entirely relevant, but I think you know the answer is that I am not entirely sure. Time passes differently when I'm stuck inside the ring."

"Well, we can always figure it out for ourselves," I said, twisting in my seat to face her. "For example, the date is the seventh of Cado, four hundred and seventy-eighth year of the Fourteenth Age."

She looked up at the ceiling as she leaned back on the bed, using her arms to prop herself up. "That would mean that... well, my memory is a bit foggy at the moment, but it would be roughly fifty-three years since I last walked free."

"Fifty years," I said in a soft breath. "That's a hell of a long time to spend all on your own."

She smiled. "Considering the average lifespan of my kind, fifty years, while not an insubstantial amount, is not overly long. I had already lived a few times that number before I was cursed."

"So, when you say your kind, you don't mean djinn, correct?" I asked, watching her thoughtfully. "You mean whatever it was that you were before."

She nodded. "Indeed. Although my people were rather scarce even before I was cursed. Fear of our magical abilities, and magical abilities in general, grew widespread. There were a few attempts at genocide over the centuries, and one finally took. Our numbers were too few to repopulate, and in the end, we dwindled away into nothingness. Only shadows of what we were, like myself and my three sisters, remain to haunt the living."

I looked down. There were more than a few genocides recorded in history. Some were regarded as heroic efforts against great evils, others as atrocities. They were all the same. Humans detested anything that was different from themselves, and needed little excuse to carry that hatred over to violence.

"I'm sorry," I whispered, lowering my head. "That can't have been easy."

Out of the corner of my eye, I could see her pull herself up straight, leaning over to gently run her fingers over my cheek. The touch sent chills down my spine, a pleasant sensation, but I tried not to focus on it.

"It isn't your fault," she said with a small smile. "Although, I do appreciate the sentiment behind it."

I shook my head, trying to change the subject away from such dark thoughts.

"So... you said your sisters were of your kind," I said, lifting my head. "But yesterday, you said that the Sisters Three weren't sisters by blood. Heh..."

"What?" Aliana asked as my voice trailed off.

"It's odd to treat the Sisters Three as fact instead of fiction, is all," I said, almost embarrassed. "Anyway, moving on. You said the three of you weren't sisters by blood. What other kind of sisters could you be?"

She nodded, turning to face me, her wings fluttering gently as she sat cross-legged on the bed. "Well, it's a little difficult to explain. The closest, I think, to something you would understand would be something like a... well, a sisterhood by oath, I suppose? But a lot more complex than that. My kind had a way to meld our minds to others that we cared about through... varying means, but it allowed us to be closer to someone we chose instead of the family we were born into. Sisters just seemed easier than having to explain all that every time."

I nodded. It did make sense. I recalled some of the mages talking about something similar. Like most nobles, they talked like people in servants' garb didn't exist until needed for some task or another, and the two men had carried the whole conversation without even noticing that I was in the room with them. I hadn't even tried to hide.

They had been talking about a mind-meld. It was difficult to create but wasn't difficult to maintain. It required a lot of artifacts to meld the minds, but maintaining it required a simple physical relationship between the two people involved. I wondered if it was the same with this meld between Aliana and her two sisters... no, it didn't seem likely. Someone as powerful as her wouldn't need something like that, right?

She was watching my reaction closely, I realized, as I'd gone silent for a long time.

"Sorry," I said quickly. "I remembered hearing some mages talking about a mind-meld like that. Apparently, it's quite difficult to create."

"For a human," she said with a chuckle.

"Fair enough," I replied with a nod.

We kept on talking as the afternoon waned and night came. She was curious about me and wanted to know what had led me to where the ring had been buried with its previous owner. It wasn't too often I had people around who wanted to hear me talk. Most of the time I was talked down to in one way or another. I had learned to take it, usually letting my mind wander, nodding and grunting at appropriate intervals to let those doing the talking know that I was at least trying to pay attention.

In this case, though, it actually seemed that she was interested in what I had to say. She stuck around even as night came and darkness required me to light a candle, asking questions and keeping my words flowing. I found myself talking about how my parents' deaths had left me in this house, stealing for Vis to earn my keep, and how the latest theft had led me to where the ring was.

Dinner was sent up to my room. Aliana had to hide for a few seconds as I collected it, but she returned quickly and eagerly. I asked if she wanted some food but she declined, telling me that Djinn didn't need any physical sustenance. It was her turn to talk as I ate.

I felt embarrassed by filling her in on my comparatively uneventful life as she started to tell me about the various conflicts she had been involved in. Apparently, her kind had inhabited places like the forest where I'd found her, in massive cities. Their magical power had been what made the humans hate them, and there had been a couple of unsuccessful attempts on her life. Some involved humans who were on her side. I wondered just how old she was and why she'd been cursed, but by the time her stories wound down, the hour was already growing late and I couldn't stop a long, jaw-splitting yawn as my last candle burned itself down to the last bit of wick.

"I think I need some sleep," I said finally, leaning back in the bed. "Do you prefer to stay here for the night?"

"That would be my preference, yes," she said with a small smile.

"Very well," I said with a chuckle. "I suppose I could set up on the floor."

"No need for that," she said quickly, laying down on the bed beside me. "Unless you feel uncomfortable sharing a bed with me?"

Uncomfortable wasn't the word, I thought as she patted the bed in front of her. There wasn't space on the bed behind her, not with her wings, which left her front the only spot available.

I shrugged as the candle sputtered out. I was too tired to dispute sharing my small bed with her, so I simply curled up next to her, pulling the blanket over both of us. Her skin was hot to the touch, I realized. Not just warm. It was on the border between pleasant and unsettling, and if any human was at that temperature, I'd tell them they were sick with a fever.

Not her though, so I decided to just enjoy the

heat of her skin pressed against mine. She leaned in, pressing a light kiss to my cheek, moving back as I turned over, almost surprised by her gesture. Pressed in close together as we were, it was all I could do not to reach out and touch her some more. From the look in her eyes, it seemed like she wanted me to do so. Instinctively, I craned my neck up, leaving my lips inches away from hers as I stared into her odd, beautiful eyes that were visible even in the dark.

The moment passed, and I dropped my head back to the bed, closing my eyes. She did the same a few seconds later, her hand running down over my side.

I shook my head. I was being stupid. Why would someone like her want to be with someone like me? I had to be just a child in her eyes, and she was only here because, by sheer chance, I had come into possession of the ring she was curse-bound to.

It was still a pleasant fantasy, I thought. Just not one to ever be entertained in the real world.

With that thought running through my head, I found myself quickly drifting off.

❧ 6 ❧

Morning came a bit too quickly. Aliana was gone by the time I woke up. I was up with the sun, as I tended to be, leaving the ring hidden under my mattress again as I headed off to get something to eat. One of the younger familiars was already waiting for me by the time I'd reached the hall where food was being served.

"Grant!" the young boy called, waving me over. "Master Vis has instructed me to guide you to him once you have finished your morning meal."

"And you're going to wait until I'm finished, are you?" I asked, filling a wooden bowl with oatmeal.

The boy nodded eagerly. I wondered if he'd eaten yet, and why he was being used to guide me. I knew every corner of this damned manor, inside and out.

I'd made a point of being extremely curious in my younger years, exploring and finding every nook and cranny that there was to be found in this damned mansion.

That said, Vis could be someplace that would require some guiding, and heavens knew that the man didn't like to be kept waiting. Either way, I wasn't going to rush my way through breakfast. I'd missed it the day before, and even though the oatmeal was a bit bland, it was still better than nothing.

As it turned out, having a guide with me hadn't been a bad call. Once I was finished with my food, the young familiar, who refused to tell me his name after I'd asked three times, guided me out of the quarters were the servants and familiars were housed, and started walking toward the path that led out of the manor, beyond the lands that were owned by Vis.

After about ten minutes of following the path deeper into the city, the boy turned off, heading toward the lake. It was rather secluded, and a very beautiful spot, I realized. I would have enjoyed it a lot more if Master Vis wasn't there waiting for me, watching me with narrowed eyes and an unreadable expression. He'd been acting strangely since the day before, and damned if I could tell what was bothering him. Was he excited? Worried? His stout, pleasant features didn't betray a single thing. I was worried that the unasked questions racing through my mind would distract me from whatever it was he wanted me to do out here.

Well, if it was magic he wanted, my being distracted wouldn't make much difference in how I performed. The man had to know by now that I was a lost cause.

"I hope you rested well and ate a hearty meal before coming to me," Vis said, gesturing for the young boy who had led me here to head back to the manor. "Your instruction today will be unlike anything you've encountered before."

I nodded. I had, against all odds, slept like a log to the point where I had even missed Aliana leaving my bed. Then again, she could slip in and out of being like a damned ghost, so that wasn't saying much.

All in all, I had rested well, and was sporting a satisfied stomach. I gave Vis a simple nod in answer to his question.

"There are various forms of magic," Vis started by saying, guiding me over to the side of the lake, where I could hear the waves lapping gently at the shoreline. "I lack the physical attributes required for the more demanding forms and so have mostly used spellcasting. It is a potent form, able, in some cases, to be the most powerful form of magic there is. There are, of course, drawbacks to its use. The more powerful the spell, the more power is required to be stored before being used, which is why for the most part I make use of familiars that allow me to keep my concentration on forming the words of power, instead of storing the power being used."

I nodded. I already knew as much, but it was nice that Vis was starting with something I was already aware of. It would make things a lot simpler when I fell flat on my face. Maybe I'd be given another afternoon off to spend with Aliana.

"Other forms of magic require more physical presence," Vis said, extending his hand to the ground. Runes on his hand started to glow and one of the rocks started to rise from the ground, stopping at about eye-level. "They are less powerful, as they require less power to use, but less time is spent gathering the power and spending it, so it is more useful in instances where one's life might be in danger."

With a flick of his wrist, the rock flew across the lake, taking a couple of skips over the water before sinking with a loud splash.

"Combat magic," I said with a nod. There had been very little instruction in that over my time here. Vis and the other tutors had said there was just so little need for those whose purpose it was to channel power to learn to use it themselves.

"Precisely," Vis said with a nod, straightening back up. "It takes a more physical toll, as you are using your body to perform the rites that your mind can do with much more competence and efficiency. Movements are required, your body acting as a mirror of your mind's will. Some of the ancients performed what they called battle dances to do their rituals. I would show you, but they were a primitive people and there is no need to carry on their legacy here."

I nodded. I would have liked to see Vis trying to dance. *Maybe some other time,* I mused.

"This is the power we will attempt to channel through you today," Vis said, pulling his cloak off, revealing that he was wearing nothing but a pair of loose pants underneath. "And we will attempt to break this annoying block that has been holding you back for such a long time."

I didn't want to tell the man that he was going to end up disappointed, but he had to know it anyway. I ground my teeth and kept my mouth shut as I moved over to join Vis on the rocky shore next to the lake.

"Now, follow my movements," Vis said, turning to face the lake, bringing his hands in fists up to his sides and bending his knees. I imitated him, feeling my body still aching from the ordeal it had been through. It was less painful now than it had been the day before, so I didn't voice any complaint. It was peaceful out here, and much more relaxing than being stuck in a room full of others who were so much more advanced than I was.

"Now, close your eyes," Vis instructed, maintaining his position a pace or so away from me. "And breathe. Focusing on bringing the air into your lungs, holding it for a second, and then releasing it. Let your mind become one with your body. Let the energy flow through you. In... hold... and out..."

I nodded, following his instructions. I had read about techniques like this before. Simple meditation moves that allowed one's body to relax and the mind to slip into a state where thoughts wouldn't plague what one was trying to accomplish. Apparently, it worked wonders for people who could already perform that kind of magic, but there had been nothing written about what it could do for someone who had no talent for this. It was frustrating.

"Focus!" Vis snapped. "I can sense your mind wandering. Think of nothing but the air rushing in and out of you. Your breathing is all you need to think of. Do not let your thoughts wander again."

The threat of pain was implied in his tone, so I did as he instructed, keeping my mind focused on the task of taking in and expelling breath.

I wasn't sure how long we spent there, knees bent, hands clenched at our sides and breathing, but when Vis finally called a halt to it, I could see that the sun was already well into its climb to the pinnacle of the sky.

Vis looked annoyed, but he didn't let it enter his

voice. A variety of different techniques were practiced as the hours wore on. Some were just simple variations of the breathing and focusing, while others seemed closer to the combat moves we had been taught before.

Following in different stances, different moves being repeated for hours and hours was a tiring prospect. Vis realized this, and eventually gave up on showing me what to do and relied simply on telling me as I moved through form after form, move after move, technique after technique until finally, as the sun was already an hour past midday, Vis called a halt.

"That is enough for today," he said, sounding almost angry. There was a look of frustration on his face as he watched me bend to lean on my knees, breathing hard. I could feel sweat starting to soak through my clothes, the only set I had for now, as the heat started to become intolerable.

I looked up after taking a few minutes to recover, to see that Vis was still eyeing me. He looked incredulous, frustrated, and more than a little angry. At me. And yet he wasn't lashing out as he normally did. Like he was expecting me to do something, and I wasn't performing the way he thought I could.

I felt a bit annoyed with myself too. The man believed in me, for some reason. While I had no idea where this faith was coming from and where it had been in the past years, I didn't want to let him down.

He had given me everything, and while I had started to pay that back by breaking the law for him, I wanted to give something back. Something more.

"We will continue this training tomorrow," Vis said, collecting his robe from the ground. "Eventually, we will find what keeps you from performing as you should, and we will overcome it. That, I promise. For now, rest and recover."

He patted me gently on the shoulder and marched off in the direction of the manor as I sat on a fallen log to catch my breath. Oddities upon oddities. He'd never been one for fatherly affection either, and now this? I shook my head. I was over-thinking this. Probably as a result of letting my mind do nothing but breathe and follow my body's movements for most of the day until now. I had followed his instructions to the letter, and with a lot more gusto than I showed to any of my other tutors.

For some reason, I had started to believe in what the man was saying. I wanted to. I needed to be something more than just the man's pet thief.

I moved over to the lake, washing my face, hands and arms in the cool, clear, refreshing water before starting the walk back to the manor.

The exercise had done wonders for my recovery, I realized. A lot of the cuts were still there, but they were healing quickly, and the bruises were starting to disappear as well. I could breathe easier, and walking was less of a limp-infused torture session.

I even let myself smile as a cool breeze cut over the lake and drifted across my face.

As I reached the manor grounds and headed toward where the servants were housed, my good mood started to evaporate. There were horses being tended to just outside the main building, and the servants were rushing about. These guests hadn't been expected, and it seemed that they had everyone on edge. I wasn't sure why, but considering what had been happening over the past couple of days, my mind did not need to leap too far to find a likely conclusion.

I caught one of the stable boys by the shoulder, dragging him to a halt as he passed me by.

"What's happening?" I asked. "Who do these horses belong to?"

"His Lordship Drake Pollock has graced us with an unannounced visit," the boy said, scowling and shaking his shoulder free from my grip. "He arrived before Master Vis did, and has been in foul spirits over having had to wait for our master to return."

"Right," I said. "Carry on, and sorry to bother you."

The boy answered with nothing but a low growl, clearly annoyed at having been interrupted in his duties by a familiar asking questions.

That said, I had little time to worry about the stable boy's problems. I had a handful of my own. Drake Pollock was the man from whom I'd stolen that magical parchment for Vis. The man was something of a favorite in the Emperor's court and wasn't likely to have bothered coming down to this manor. The more likely course of action would have been to send a letter asking Master Vis to join him at his manse. Vis would have jumped at the opportunity to rub elbows with the man and his peers.

Which begged the question, why was Pollock here? I doubted it was my fault. There was no reason why they would know that I was Vis' man. Even though the Lancers and mercenaries had gotten a good look of my face, it had been dark, and they didn't know me from the Emperor himself. And the way that I had escaped their clutches couldn't have been tracked, right?

Right?

Well, there was only one person to ask who would know any real answer to that question, and that person was currently confined to a dull bronze ring hidden under my mattress.

I moved quickly into the servants' house, trying not to seem like I was rushing as I moved through the building. I took the steps up to my room two at a time, pushing the door open and closing it behind me, careful to slide the bolt closed before moving over to my bed.

I pulled the ring out and rubbed it urgently, looking around. She *had* disappeared into the ring, hadn't she? She could have gone exploring too, I supposed. She knew how to travel from one point to another in a second's time, after all, so she could be anywhere. I could be rubbing a useless piece of jewelry for all I knew.

"What do you--?"

"Oh fuck!" I quickly snapped around. "Must you do that every damn time?"

"No," she said with a grin. "But it's fun to watch you jump like that every time." She paused, seeing how agitated I looked. "Is everything all right?"

"I don't know," I said, softly, moving over to sit on the bed. "The man I stole that parchment from is here, and from the looks of things, he's not too happy about it."

Aliana nodded, moving over to me and taking a seat on the bed instead of kneeling at my feet. I took a moment to smile and appreciate that. She noticed and smirked.

"I could probably bring you over to listen in on what Pollock is talking about with Vis," she said softly. "In fact, I could show you how to use that power yourself, if you wish it."

I opened my mouth but didn't say anything for a

moment. If you wish it, she'd said. Sure, the djinn of stories were the kind that offered wishes to those that held their objects of power, but after our talk the night before, I had somehow lost track of the fact that she was indeed a djinn. The way she'd said it, it felt like she was offering something, a djinn to her master, and it was something of a jolt.

"Look," I finally said, turning to face her. "I don't want it to seem like I'm taking advantage of you, or your powers. As useful as that would be right now, I don't want to abuse it. You've helped me a lot already, even so far as saving my life back in those caves, and I want you to know that I'm grateful and fully intend on repaying that debt somehow. That debt, and any other I might incur if you help me further."

She paused, looking at me oddly. I couldn't tell if she was surprised or annoyed by what I'd said. What I could tell was that she was thinking her words through carefully, not wanting to rush into a response.

I could understand that, I supposed. I was suddenly rethinking a couple of things I'd just said myself. Debt? How was I ever going to pay her back for saving my life? It wasn't like she needed my help for anything, anyway.

"You should know that you owe me no debt, Grant," she said with a smile, turning to fully face me. "You saved my life by dragging me out of that damned ring as much as I did by removing you from the clutches of the men who had you bound. However, if you do wish this to be a gift-exchanging kind of relationship, know that if I help you, you can help me as well."

"How?" I asked, leaning closer.

"If you help me track down my sisters, find them wherever they've been lost or secreted themselves in the world, I will help you in return," she said, her voice low and thoughtful. "I will help you attain your power. Your true power. The kind that neither you, nor even your master, has ever dreamed of."

"Come on, not this again," I said. "I've just spent the whole fucking day trying to convince Vis that there's no latent power inside of me, and now I have to convince you, too?"

She smirked. "I know for a fact that what you just said isn't true," she whispered, leaning closer to me. Close enough that I could feel the heat radiating from her body as my eyes seemed to get lost in hers. "Help me, and I'll show you just how wrong you are."

I looked toward the door, grinding my teeth. Well, if there was anyone in the world who could dig up some kind of power inside me, she would be my top choice. If only it meant that I was spending time near the lake with her instead of Vis. I gazed down at my lap for a moment as I gathered my courage, then looked up at her, steadily keeping my eyes from staring too long at the breasts that were almost hanging out of her 'clothes'.

I offered her my hand. "That's a deal."

She looked down at it questioningly.

"You grab it, and shake it," I explained hurriedly.

"Oh," she said with a laugh, taking my hand in hers then gripping it tightly and shaking it.

❧ 7 ❧

I honestly wasn't sure what I'd just agreed to.
There had been a promise of greater powers than
I'd ever dreamed of, but since I'd never even considered there might be powers in my future, that bar was
set pretty damned low.

As the moment of silence carried on until it
started to become awkward, I looked at the woman
who wasn't a human woman sitting next to me. There
was something about her. She exuded a kind of infec-
tious passion. I wasn't sure if that was the reason why
I agreed to help her in finding her sisters, or if I actually thought it was a good idea.

The thought that I might be doing this because of
a more carnal urge occurred to me as well. She was
beautiful. Sure, there were more than enough oddities. She had horns, green hair, and her skin was a

slightly different shade than I'd ever seen in humans before. But there was no denying that she was beautiful. Maybe not in spite of those characteristics, but partly because of them.

I realized I was staring and quickly looked away. There was nothing to see, really, so my eyes instead moved down to where my hands were balled into fists on my lap.

"So, what do we have to do to start looking for your sisters?" I asked, realizing that it had been a while since either of us spoke.

"We have to go to back the tomb where you found me," Alianna said softly as she caught my gaze and held it. "There's something about the dead woman that is calling to my mind and I can't push it away. I know she's important, but I'm not sure why."

I nodded, leaning forward. "Well, if we're heading back there, I'd really rather not do that transport thing you did that got us out of there."

"Why not?" she asked, sounding annoyed. "It's much faster than walking or riding, and we wouldn't have to worry about being discovered on the way."

"And it feels like my head is being cut in half with a butcher's cleaver," I added, grinding my teeth at the memory. "While I realize it was a necessity that time, and infinitely preferable to what I assume actually having my head cut in two by a cleaver would be like, I was hoping we could avoid it this time."

Aliana inhaled deeply, like she was keeping herself from trying to convince me to do it anyway. I was glad she didn't try, since that would have gotten me to cave fairly quickly. I did want to impress her.

"Fine," she finally agreed with a deep sigh. "But I hope you realize that means we'll have to wait until nightfall. It's not like I can just walk around in broad daylight. Turning heads is precisely what you don't need right now."

"Why can't I just put you back in the ring?" I asked, glancing down at it then back up at her.

"Besides the fact that being encased in a piece of jewelry is more painful than your head being split in two, not to mention demeaning?" she asked, unconsciously drawing back. "What if you need my help? What if someone sees and recognizes you? What happens then? Are you going to find the ring and rub it while being chased through the city streets?"

"I'll have you know that I can be rather hard to catch," I said quickly, in a defensive voice. Even so, she had a point. I'd rather not have to call her out of the ring again should trouble arise. It looked like we were going to wait until night fell, when she would look less conspicuous.

I'd have to find some sort of cloak for her, however. There was no amount of darkness that would hide the fact that there were horns coming out from the top of her head.

I leaned back onto the bed, closing my eyes for a moment. We had time to kill, I supposed, and there was a beautiful... djinn in my bed. Wishes and the possibilities that came with them were vivid in my mind, and it was all I could do not to open my eyes and try to make it so. The thought of having her slap me for even thinking such a thing was terrifying, though. It never occurred to me that she might say yes.

Why would she? For all I knew, we might not even be compatible in that fashion.

I opened my eyes to see her staring at me, like she knew what I was thinking. There was a bemused expression on her face, made better by the slight tilt of her head that sent her long hair drifting down over her shoulder. It was all I could do not to reach out and touch it, just to see if it was as soft as it looked.

She smiled, like she could see that thought too, and I quickly turned away. From the way the light was fading from the open window, I could tell that night would be falling soon. I wondered if Vis would send someone up with some dinner, since he probably didn't want me wandering around the property with Pollock still around.

The thought of him coming to my room or sending someone to find me and discovering that I wasn't there was something of a distracting thought, and one that I was having trouble consolidating.

There were no slaves in the Empire since that had been forbidden years before, and yet a good amount of the practices remained firmly in place with only the name by which they were known, changing. People weren't slaves anymore, but servants. And while technically free, they owed service for their food and board, and the payment for that could be taken out in a variety of ways, only one of which was labor.

I smirked. These were dark thoughts, but at least they were a better choice than thinking about what Aliana looked like minus her skimpy clothes.

Damn. Now my mind was drawn back to that.

A few hours passed as the sun dropped lower, almost completely disappearing from sight. Aliana had to disappear into the ring for a moment as a servant came to my door with a tray of food for the evening meal, as I'd suspected. Vis made no such appearance. As the servant left, I quickly found a clean bag and stored the apple, bread, dried meat and hard cheese that had been sent up. Hardly a feast, but I assumed the cooks had been occupied by preparing meals for the unexpected company, leaving us to have cold leftovers.

It was something to be expected, I realized, but not really something I enjoyed.

Aliana eyed me curiously as I stored the food for later.

"What?" I asked, grinning a bit shamefully. "I'm no djinn. I'll be hungry later, and do not intend to spend the rest of the night with a rumbling stomach."

She raised her hands quickly. "I didn't say anything."

"Good," I grunted with a nod, putting the food into the pack I was quickly preparing. New candles, my flint and striking steel, some rope, and a fresh set of clothes. There was no telling if there was going to be any tearing and ripping, and I wanted to be prepared for that this time.

I opened my door quietly, stepping out and listening for any movements. What few servants were still on duty would be restricted to the manor. The rest would be heading off to sleep, which meant there wouldn't be much in the way of people for us to run into.

There was no sense in leaving anything to chance, though, so as we moved out I turned to Aliana, who was following close behind me.

"I don't suppose you'd have any tricks up your sleeve that would keep us from sight, would you?" I asked in a hushed whisper.

She smiled. "I already put a field of sorts to keep us hidden from anyone except those who might actually be looking for us."

"Oh. How does that work?" I asked as I waited for her to quietly close the door behind us.

"Well, it only works if you keep your voice down, and otherwise try to avoid drawing attention to yourself," she said softly, moving closer to me. Close enough that I could feel the heat emanating from her body. "It alters the perception of others, helping them ignore us unless they step into the field. I suggest we avoid that at all costs."

"Good idea," I replied, nodding. I wasn't sure what the hell she was talking about. I'd never heard of any spells that altered perception, since that would require reaching into the mind of every single person we encountered and pushing their attention away from us. As such, it was theoretically possible, but very, very impractical.

Then again, nobody was really sure what a djinn would be capable of, since less than a week before, I would not have been blamed for assuming that djinn were a fictional race.

I assumed that the world was full of similar surprises. In this case, it was pleasant.

As we moved through the courtyard, I could see a couple of servants moving quickly across the cobbles. Whether they were only in a rush, or if Aliana's magic was working, I didn't know. Either way, it seemed that we had a clear way to the city when I suddenly paused in my tracks. So suddenly that Aliana didn't notice and crashed into me from behind. We didn't make a sound, but as I staggered, twisting to face her and regain my balance, I realized that my hands had gone to her waist and pulled her closer to me.

The sudden distraction was not something that was needed at the moment and I gave her a moment to move away before relaxing again and facing front.

"Sorry about that." I rubbed gently at my arm.

"Stay focused," she said. "Why did you stop?"

I didn't reply, not wanting to say another word as the large, wooden doors to the main house swung open. Pollock marched out quickly, Master Vis following close at his heels.

"You don't understand," Vis was saying, but was cut off as Pollock raised his hand.

"I understand perfectly, Vis." He indicated for his retinue to start preparing the horses for departure. "Your actions have been suspect for far too long, with far too little consequence. I think it high time to address that injustice."

"I have done nothing. I swear it!" Vis answered, his voice taking on a whiny, apologetic quality I'd heard him use when he was trying to appeal to some-one's better nature. It usually worked, but it wasn't often plied on a man as angry as Pollock appeared to be.

"That will be for the Official to decide," Pollock snarled, turning back to face Vis down. Vis, a good few inches shorter than Pollock, quickly shied away like a hound fearing the whip.

"The Official?" Vis asked. For the first time since I knew the man, I could see a crack in his outer shell of a smooth, silver-tongued negotiator and saw the coward underneath.

Well, not really a coward, I mused. You didn't have to be a coward to fear the wrath of the man who commanded the Emperor's Lancers. The stories went that the Official had some magical ability of his own, but nobody had ever been able to prove it. All those who would have been privy to such a demonstration rarely escaped it with their lives.

I reached behind myself instinctively, taking Aliana's hand and squeezing it. It was more for my assurance than hers, since I doubted she knew who the Official was.

"Your wards are far too powerful for someone of your lowly station," Pollock said, looking around himself, like he could see the runes that had been woven into the air around him. "And far too powerful for someone of your insubstantial power. You will kneel here in the courtyard and await the Official's arrival. I would warn you against running, but I would be amused if you attempted it."

Pollock's horse, a massive, muscular black stallion, was brought around and the man quickly mounted, cruelly digging his heels into the beast's flanks and driving him forward.

"Fucking cunt," I heard Vis say, but even as Pollock rode away with the rest of his retinue, Vis looked around, his face red with anger and shame as he dropped, first to one knee and then the second. The servants that still remained in the area quickly backed away and out of sight. If Vis survived his encounter with the Official, there was little doubt he would want as few witnesses to his humiliation as possible.

"Let's go," I whispered, tugging Aliana toward the gate that had been left open. We slipped outside without attracting any attention, heading toward the forest. I suddenly realized that while I was staunch in my determination not to be ported back to the ruins, I actually had no idea where they were. When encountering them for the first time, I had been running for my life and had little time to inspect my surroundings or maintain a sense of direction of where I was going. And we had left using another path, somehow. I still wasn't sure how Aliana had brought us away from them. Portals, again, were hypothetically possible, but unreliable and very difficult to maintain. There were written accounts of mages who had made the attempt with only a modicum of success. Their failed attempts ended poorly. Some were lost forever while others arrived in different locations than intended, while still others arrived where intended, only to find that their legs, arms and sometimes even heads had ended up elsewhere.

Djinn were very interesting, and I vowed to take the time to ask and learn from Aliana when all this was finished.

As I thought about it, I had the idea of heading back to Pollock's mansion, circling around to the forest behind it and trying to find my way in that fashion. I didn't want to explain my process to Aliana, of course, since she would discard it and portal us to the ruins directly. As I recalled from the last time, it wasn't like she really needed my permission to do so.

I wondered why she hadn't just gone ahead and done it despite my protests and put that thought down with all the rest of the questions that I was storing for later. I needed some material to help our conversations flow a bit more. As we'd run out of things to say about ourselves, I found that more and more annoying silences popped up.

Only I could make a conversation with a newly-discovered race boring. I shook my head gently, keeping my eyes focused on the growing crowd I could see as we got closer to Pollock's mansion. I wasn't sure what it was for, but the fact remained that if the idea wasn't to be seen, a crowd could be a boon or a curse. That many people would mask us from eyes that might recognize us, but it would also increase the number of said eyes. And what was worse, Aliana had said that people could not intrude on the field she'd created, which meant that we would have to stay far away from all the people in the crowd while trying to stay as inconspicuous as possible.

And at that moment I realized I'd completely forgotten to grab a cloak to help cover Aliana's horns.

We really needed to let her field of whatever it was do its work, or we would be caught the moment someone saw her.

As we moved closer to the crowd, what they were congregated for quickly became clearer. The Official was almost as rare a sight to see in the city as the Emperor himself, and when he appeared, there were always people who either wanted to see a novelty or plead some sort of case before him. There had been no record of the man ever taking notice of such appeals, but that didn't stop them from trying.

There was already a group of Lancers waiting on horseback outside. I'd always liked horses and found myself distracted by the sight of the magnificent beasts. Powerful warhorses weren't pets and could be almost as violent as war dogs, but were cared for with a great deal of affection by their riders. And it showed.

They quickly parted as the sight of a man in black

plate and no helmet, identifiable by the heavy beard and long, flowing hair he sported, drew their attention. I could see Pollock, still on horseback, waiting impatiently behind the man. As we drew closer, I could hear what was being said.

"You overstep, Pollock," the Official said in an impressively deep voice.

"The man is a base thief and a coward," Pollock said, still in a foul mood. I wondered if this was something new due to the theft, or if he was just always in a bad mood. "Why the Emperor would accept him into the gentry eludes me, but I would never question the Emperor's decisions," Pollock added that last part when the Official turned and hit him with a glare that proved once and for all that looks couldn't kill.

"You would do well to remember that," the armored man growled.

"I did no wrong," Pollock said defensively. "My loyalty to the emperor is as it always has been. Why would I be responsible?"

"It isn't important," The Official said, flipping his hair back behind his shoulder again. "I will find the truth of the matter myself. Be assured, any parties responsible will suffer."

I gulped. Sure, the veiled threat hadn't been directed at me, but then again, it really had. There wasn't any escaping the fact that I was one of the responsible parties.

Aliana tugged gently at my arm, dragging me clear of the courtyard and into some bushes.

"What?" I whispered urgently. "We can't stay here too long."

"Agreed," she said, taking a firm grip on my hand. "However, we tried it your way and almost ended up caught by this Official of yours. I apologize for the pain to your head but..."

"No, no, no," I tried to say, my voice rising for an instant before I felt like I'd just been sucked through a hole. The sensation knocked the breath out of my chest, sending my vision swirling with unintentional tears as I dropped to my knees, gasping for air. For a second, it seemed like there wasn't any result, until finally it took, and I dropped onto my back on the ground, coughing softly.

The ground, as it turned out, was a hard stone floor instead of soft grass. The sight that greeted me as I looked up was simple blackness instead of the bright moon and stars.

And my head was pounding like it was an anvil being beaten by a blacksmith's hammer. It seemed as though the portal had worked after all.

"Fuck," I finally managed to say, turning over to the only light source in the room, Aliana's horns.

"I'm sorry," she said, looking back at me and smiling apologetically. "But if I had allowed you to have a say, you would have raised your voice and we would have been caught."

"Fuck," I repeated, turning over onto my stomach and pushing myself to my knees. The pain had spread down my back and all over my body. I wondered if this was what being struck by lightning felt like.

After a few long, terrifying seconds, I managed to push myself to my feet, closing my eyes and trying to still my suddenly queasy stomach.

"How do you get used to this?" I wondered aloud.

Aliana took it like I'd been talking with her and turned to face me. "I honestly have no idea what you're talking about. Then again, I've never stepped through a portal with a human before. I'll need to investigate it further. Unfortunately, further investigation would require you to go through the portals with me a few more times."

"I can't wait," I muttered, steadying myself on the pedestal that held the coffin we were looking at.

Aliana was rummaging around with the dead body inside. Interestingly enough, even after two more days, the body still looked slightly dead. Like she'd only died a few hours ago. I made a face, trying to understand just what could do this to a body, and why someone would even want it done to a vessel they weren't inhabiting anymore.

I was young, and the concept of death had only

just started to make itself painfully aware in my consciousness.

"So," I said. "Are you the one responsible for this?" I gestured to the body.

"She was the last one to hold my ring," Aliana said softly.

"And you killed her for it?" I asked.

"No," she said with a shrug. "I didn't stop it from happening. I can't actually kill someone who holds my ring. If you own the ring, you own me. As your slave, in a way."

"Well, that's not at all the same thing," I grumbled, rubbing at my temple. "Thanks for making me realize I might be next in line to have my death go unprevented." There were issues other than my pending mortality, of course. I knew what it was like to be a slave in a way, as she said, and I wouldn't wish it on anyone much less own a slave myself.

She turned to face me. With the soft light from her horns, I could see her smiling in that cocky way she had. As she came closer, I was suddenly very aware of how hot her skin was. Mostly because it was suddenly pressed against mine. I was a few inches taller than she was, so I could feel her breasts pushing into my chest. Though what she was wearing looked metallic, it turned out to be perfectly malleable and very thin—as I discovered when I felt her nipples pressing to my chest.

"I... well," I tried to say, but stopped when she placed her finger over my lips.

"Well, I am your slave now," she whispered, angling her head up and leaning in close enough that I could feel her lips moving over the bare skin of my neck. "But it could be so much better." She emphasized the last three words by pressing her body tighter against mine, one of her legs coming up to run up and down the side of my leg. "Our relationship could be very transformative for you."

My mouth was dry, and I was very aware of how little her clothes were actually covering. I opened my mouth a few times but failed to produce any words as I realized that there were more reactions to her actions. Somehow, I completely forgot we were in the middle of abandoned ruins, inside a mausoleum and actually standing right next to an open casket. All that flew right out of my mind as she started to grind into me, pressing harder against me as I grew large enough to push against her hip.

"How?" I asked before I could stop myself.

She pulled away, and I could see her grinning at me, running her hand up my shoulder, ending at my chin and tilting my head to look her in the eyes, as mine had drifted down to where one of her breasts had escaped her clothes.

My eyes adjusted to the darkness and I could see

her grinning unabashedly when my gaze drifted back up.

"I could break free, but the ring dampens my latent power. If we find my sisters, my power will be rather magnified," she said with a chuckle. "Also, sex —for my kind, anyway—is one of the ultimate displays of trust, and trust means sharing of power. And I did promise you power, didn't I?"

A rushing sound filled my ears. As she talked about sex, it was all I could do not to lean closer, wanting to hear more. I gulped, and her grin grew larger.

I wasn't sure if she was propositioning me or not. I wasn't wholly experienced in the area, so she could be, or she could just be making conversation about what her people were like while trying to convince me to rid her of the ring, maybe? Even so, I couldn't deny that I was tempted. Sure, with the horns and the wings she wasn't what one might call a classical beauty, but there *was* beauty, and a lot of it, on display. For someone like me, who hadn't had much of a physical relationship except with myself, that was definitely on my mind.

But this was something different. There seemed to be two options in my mind. Either she was only acting this way because I was the one who owned the ring and she saw me as some kind of master over her, or she was trying to gain an advantage that would leave me in a coffin like the woman behind me.

I gently pushed her arm to the side and moved out from between her and the pedestal, shaking my head.

"I think we need to move," I said, my voice sounding hoarse and throaty. "There have to be people still patrolling or watching this place. It's not smart to stay here if we don't have to."

It was hard to tell in the meagre light, but there was a crestfallen appearance to her face as she nodded, reaching into the coffin and quickly pulling a pouch from the dead woman's waist.

"Then we should go," Aliana said, forcing a smile.

❧ 8 ❧

It was nice to be with someone who had at least a middling sense of direction. The last time I was here, I wasn't entirely sure how I was going to make it out. The place was a damned maze that had apparently been built long ago and added onto for centuries, as it went on and on. And yet, Aliana seemed to know her way through these abandoned tunnels, making for a much smoother go of it.

She took the lead, winding us through the narrow corridors and hallways. I didn't want to ask her why we weren't teleporting away. If the thought just hadn't occurred to her, maybe my bringing it up would put it in her mind again and I'd have to deal with even more of the pain that was still making my head pound like a drum.

All that said, I couldn't help heaving a sigh of

relief as we stepped out of the tunnels, leaving the musky, damp air behind, with a fuller, fresher, if slightly warmer replacement filling our lungs.

"Not keen on tunnels, are you?" Aliana asked with a chuckle.

"Not really," I admitted. "Though that might be because I was almost carried away for torture and death the last time I was here. I'll figure it out eventually."

Aliana smirked, but her smile quickly disappeared. I could tell why only a few seconds later, as the sound of heavy boots tromping over dried leaves and fallen branches could be heard, approaching us from all sides.

"How could they know we're here?" I wondered aloud, already knowing the answer. Wards had been set to keep away intruders, and when Aliana teleported us in, it must have triggered some sort of warning to the men set to guard the place. When we exited the tunnels, they knew where we were and approached with caution.

"Hey now, I know you," I heard a familiar voice say as its owner stepped out of the shadows. Kruger's face was a hard one to forget even in the most pleasant of circumstances. As it stood between us, the looming moonlight filtering through the trees and stone archway made it difficult not to remember the last time we'd seen each other.

I turned to see Aliana wasn't beside me anymore. I gritted my teeth in protest. If there was ever a time to transport me against my will, this was it, and now was when she decided to part ways? I remembered what she said about not killing her previous owner and wondered if this was her way of not preventing my death.

It made sense. I'd want out from under my figurative heel as well.

"We've got you this time, you thieving little twerp," Kruger said as five more men slipped out from the underbrush, all looking rather hostile, like they were about to redecorate the abandoned ruins with my insides.

Kruger looked like he was going to get the first try as he started moving forward. My mind was working at an impossible pace, making it seem like the heavy, lead-weighted cudgel he was carrying moved slowly toward my skull. There were too many of them to evade. I'd only gotten away the last time by the element of surprise and more than a little luck, which wasn't going to be playing in my favor now. They could all see me and were otherwise unimpeded in reaching me. I could avoid Kruger and maybe one or two more, but the rest would swarm me before I could make it to the woods and that would be the end of it.

I realized that as I overanalyzed the situation,

Kruger's cudgel hadn't stopped moving and was approaching my head with alarming speed. Even as I thought about that, I froze. My brains being spread across the stones around me was a very compelling image in my mind's eye, and yet it failed to move me to action. It was all going to end badly anyway. Why should I prolong the suffering? At least this way, I wouldn't be tortured into revealing that Vis was the mastermind behind all this.

I forced myself to keep my eyes open as I watched the top-heavy cudgel sailing toward my unprotected head. My eyes opened wider when the weapon suddenly stopped in midair. Kruger looked almost as stupefied as I was, as we turned in unison to see what had stopped him. There was a hand gripping it. A woman's hand.

Well, not really a woman, a small, annoying part of my mind corrected as I saw Aliana standing there. Her face was filled with a fury that I thought looked very foreign on her as she twisted the cudgel back around, taking the power of it away from Kruger, who had very little to say as she hammered it into his gut then tilted it up, crunching the top-heavy weapon into his face. The force of the blow knocked him clean off his feet, leaving him facing the sky and groaning softly in pain, his mouth and nose both broken and leaking blood.

The surprise faded from the other five, who

quickly hefted their weapons. None had a sword, since their jobs never called for it, but clubs and maces were produced as they collectively roared in defiance of the winged, horned woman in front of them.

As the world slowly came back into full motion, there was a part of me that really wanted to admire what I was watching. I had spent hundreds of hours being taught how to fight, how to evade, and how to win, but it all seemed so pointless, watching her go through the motions of combat. She looked like she was dancing, even as she stole a weapon from the man in front of her and turned it on him, hitting him with it again and again until he stumbled back, spitting blood and teeth.

It was beautiful and horrifying at the same time. I wondered at how easy it was to consolidate the two. There was a part of me that wanted to help. Even with the wings and the horns there was something about her that brought my mind to protecting her, keeping her from harm.

Then again, I realized that I never needed to worry. She could take care of herself, and she could do it a hell of a lot better than I could. As it turned out, she was the one protecting me from harm.

I could handle myself, of course. I hadn't spent years being taught how to evade and fight back for nothing, after all. That said, six battle-hardened mercenaries with clubs were beyond anything I could do.

Not beyond anything she could do, apparently, as the last man dropped to the ground with a crunch of broken bones. There was a flicker as steel caught and reflected the light of the moon and stars as Aliana produced a knife. It looked intricate and beautifully crafted, so it clearly wasn't something she'd picked up off the downed men in front of her.

I opened my mouth to ask her to stop, but hesitation struck me like a blow to the stomach. Did I want her to stop? What had they done to deserve having their lives spared?

I blinked as her blade quickly rose and fell, opening a long and very lethal wound on the man's neck. He coughed, choked and dropped back to the ground, clutching futilely at the wound, but quickly lost focus on the task as he bled out in seconds.

A few of the men rose from the beautiful beating that had just been laid on them. I couldn't tell if it was to continue the fight or run away. It didn't really matter, since Aliana was on them, a flurry of wings and knives. Blood dribbled from heavy wounds as the three remaining men dropped to their knees, grunting and screaming in pain.

I didn't realize how dry my eyes were from staring with mouth-gaping awe at what I'd just seen, trying to understand it. Her blade was dripping red gore, but there was only a splatter of it on her cheek, which she quickly cleaned with an annoyed huff.

"Are you all right?" she asked, beaming with pride as she offered me her hand. I wondered why for a moment before seeing that I'd dropped down onto the flagstones in shock.

"Are you?" I whispered incredulously, blinking a few times and snapping my jaw shut. "What did you just do?"

"I saved your life?" she answered, sounding confused. "You see this as a good thing, yes? Because I could have just let him crack your skull open with that primitive weapon of his."

"Well, yes, all fine and good," I said, trying not to stammer, suddenly feeling a very reasonable terror regarding the woman in front of me. I took her hand and she pulled me to my feet in a smooth motion.

"You sound less than satisfied, though," she said softly, tilting her head in inquiry. "What's the matter?"

"You just killed them," I whispered. "Where did you learn to do that?"

"I told you I fought in a war, Grant," she said, still eyeing me curiously. "You know I was no shield-maiden or nurse. What did you think I did?"

She had a point, but I still had a lot of unprocessed emotion to deal with.

"Why did you kill them?" I asked.

"Because they were trying to kill you," Aliana replied, starting to sound more annoyed than confused now.

"Well, yes," I huffed. "But you could have left them disarmed, unable to keep us from escaping. Now you have just added murder to the crimes the Official will be laying at my feet. I'm a dead man. So fucking dead."

"You should know there were deaths when I got you out of here the first time," Aliana said softly. "Or did you think I would allow those... Lancers, did you call them? Did you think I would have allowed them to take word back to your Official about my part in all this?"

I opened my mouth to answer, but again, she made a good point. I could only imagine the kind of destruction that would be raining down if the Official, and the Emperor in turn, found that there was a djinn living among them.

Aliana rolled her eyes and dropped to the ground, wiping her blade clean on Kruger's sleeve.

"I'm not some evil demon in need of death or destruction, Grant," she said quietly, not looking me in the eye as she spoke. "I'll just do anything to keep you alive. Anything to protect you, now that you hold my ring. Besides..." she added with a small smirk, "I'd rather you not die before we have a chance to be intimate."

"You think now is the best time to proposition me?" I asked, raising an eyebrow. "Right now?"

She shrugged. "It's part of my nature. And something you might want to get used to if we spend more time together."

Any other time, any other place, and I would have been open to getting used to Aliana making advances toward me. That said, I had just watched her massacre a gauntlet of mercenaries requiring very few weapons and no armor. She didn't even need clothes, I realized. Not much of them, at least.

Once she was finished cleaning her blade, she looked up at me with an odd, indecipherable expression before searching through Kruger's clothes, pulling out a small pouch that jingled like it had coins in it. She tossed it to me, not even looking up to see if I'd caught it before moving on to the others. More coins and small trinkets presented themselves, but nothing of true value until Aliana squeaked excitedly. It was a sound I'd never heard from her before, and likely never would again.

It was enough to draw my attention, though. As I moved closer, I could see her polishing what looked like a small glass globe, about the size of an apple. As trinkets went it was actually one of the nicer ones, and judging by Aliana's excitement, she seemed to think it wasn't just some bauble.

She held it up for me to see. "It's a looking orb.

Well, it could be, if I can get it to work again. Lost in the hands of some brute, it might have inherited some of his dullard attitudes and become useless... come on... there we go!" She grinned broadly as the glass inside the orb started to swirl, giving the impression that it was full of tiny stars.

"Show me Norel," she whispered. I could see runes rising from her arms as she ran her fingers over the glass. The stars began spinning at a faster speed and continued accelerating until they were all blurred together. As they did, a shape started to form. It was just a face at first. As the stars started spinning faster, colors and a background started to form. The face was of a woman with features similar to Aliana's, talking with someone else. A noble, by the look of his robes. I couldn't hear what they were saying, but from the confused look on Aliana's face, I could tell that she could.

"That's the guard building," I said as I continued watching.

"How do you know?" Aliana asked, not looking up from the orb.

"Suffice it to say that I've been inside it before," I said softly, not wanting to get into the details of what I'd done for Vis when I'd found my way inside the guardhouse. "She's talking with Lord Kallaghen, one of the Emperor's advisors."

"I don't believe her," Aliana said. "She's acting as a

noble and seems to be mixed up in the politics of this realm. Damn her."

"Oh, shit." I dropped down next to Aliana on the ground, not caring overmuch that there was blood starting to seep into my clothes. "What you're telling me is that your sister is a noblewoman, and one of pretty high standing from the looks of things. And to find her, we'll have to either get into the guard building or track her down at home, all while evading Master Vis, Pollock, and the Official. Have I missed anything?"

Aliana turned to me, narrowing her eyes and tilting her head. "As I saw it, your master is something of a lesser noble, a new addition to the gentry, but he seems like he might be able to help us track my sister down. We can use his connections to help find her. In addition, we can take advantage of that and keep an eye on what Pollock and the Official are conspiring."

I nodded. "After all this, we're just heading back to the manor and hoping Vis hasn't noticed that I left?"

"Well, as I understand it, he's either still on his knees outside the building or otherwise occupied," Aliana said with a smile. "I think he has more important things on his mind than to keep track of one of his familiars."

"Good point," I conceded. "Though... what

happens if the guards find out we're responsible for what happened here?"

Aliana smiled, shaking her head. "If you know me by now, you should know that there is no way for a human to discover a djinn's fresh kill."

"I'm finding that there are more things to discover about you by the hour," I said with a chuckle. "I don't feel like walking all the way back to the manor."

"Say no more," Aliana grinned, standing up and tucking her knife and the orb into her clothes, though I wasn't sure where, as there didn't seem to be any space for that kind of storage. Either way, I had little time to investigate as she gripped both my hands. In the blink of an eye, I found myself being dragged through what felt like a minuscule hole. It was difficult to explain, but there was a twisting, twirling sensation that knocked the breath out of me. I couldn't inhale for the duration and found myself coughing and choking once we came out of it.

There were no lights, but the comfortable and familiar surroundings quickly told me that we were back in my room. I opened my mouth to say something foul but realized that Aliana was nowhere to be seen. She'd arrived in the room. I knew that much, having heard her walking around the room, but now she had slipped into the ring, I supposed? I wasn't entirely sure how she managed it.

After a few seconds of listening, I realized there was someone bounding up the steps to my room. She had clearly heard it and slipped away, out of sight. I would have to ask her if it was because djinn just had better hearing, or some other magical reason.

It didn't matter for the moment, however. I quickly found myself drawn to my feet as the door burst open. Even in the dim light, I could see Master Vis standing there. He'd just come from brighter surroundings so it took him a moment to find me in the darkness, but once he did, he grabbed me by the collar.

"You need to come with me, now." He sounded anxious and upset, displaying the same flustered qualities that had made me wonder what was bothering him before, in much greater scale.

I nodded, quickly following in his footsteps as he released my shirt collar. He hadn't noticed the red that had soaked into my grey robes, or if he had, he made no mention of it as we started heading toward the mansion at full speed.

❧ 9 ❧

I felt stupid for following Vis so blindly and without asking any questions. I doubted that they would be answered anyway but as he led me to the manor's cellars, I realized that had to be one of the dumbest things I had done all day. Considering how my day had gone, that bar was set rather high.

Once I'd stepped inside, he had locked the door behind me and left without another word, leaving me with no light and a veritable horde of questions but not a single answer in sight. With Vis and the only source of light gone, I found myself alone in what could only be described as a small dungeon to stew over what could be going on. Had he noticed my absence? Was he punishing me for it? No, that wasn't likely. He liked to make his examples very visible and obvious to all those who might want to make similar mistakes. I ground my teeth, trying to come up with some sort of answer, but nothing concrete displayed itself. I thought of calling Aliana up. The ring was still in my pocket. Vis hadn't even bothered to take away my pack, I realized.

No, best not, I mused. I didn't know how long I was going to be down here, or who might be watching. I could afford to wait and see what was going to happen. If things started to go badly, I could summon her to make mincemeat of everyone around here as well.

I dropped onto the small cot that had been provided in the room, rubbing my temples and pushing the effects of the portal out of my mind as much as I could. My head was pounding, and it seemed to only get worse every time we used it. Aliana had no idea what caused the damn headaches and was therefore of little help.

I perked up when I heard the sound of footsteps approaching the cell I was being held in. The sight of flickering torchlight made me hope there might be someone that could let me out, or at least get me some water, but instead, it was Vis. He had the same crazed, flustered look about him, though it seemed to be more under control at the moment.

Keys jangled in the lock, quickly opening it as Vis pushed inside, closing the door behind him.

"Listen to me," Vis said, his voice a low growl,

kind of like the low rumble that slowly built into thunder. "Listen carefully, as I detest repeating myself. I need you to tell me what happened that night at Pollock's house. I need you to be thorough, and entirely honest. Any discrepancy in what you tell me will be punished severely. Do you understand?"

I ground my teeth and nodded. I wasn't sure I trusted Vis not to turn me in to the Official to save his own skin, and therefore had no intention of telling him the full story willingly. That didn't mean that he wouldn't be able to drag it out me unwillingly, but this time I was going to make him work for it. I wasn't some lamb to be fed to a lion as sacrifice.

"I broke into the noble's house, as you ordered," I started. "I found the parchment you wanted me to bring back, but when I picked it up off the pedestal it was on, I must have triggered some kind of ward, since there were guards on me seconds later. I managed to evade them, but more started coming as I made my way out. I was slowed down by some sort of protection field that was trying to keep the parchment from leaving the property. I started running into the woods behind the mansion. The guards were hot on my trail, of course, but I found some ruins inside the woods, and by navigating them, I was able to elude my would-be captors and make my way here. I didn't want to be seen entering the premises under suspicious circumstances, so I snuck in and climbed up through my window, which I left open, just in case."

I'd delivered the whole of the story in a firm monotone, keeping my eyes glued to the ground as a good servant would while talking to his master. There was a lot to hide in my story, but I'd become something of an accomplished liar over the years. I only hoped those skills weren't failing me now.

Vis gripped the sides of my head with both hands, lifting my head to look him in the eyes. There was a mask of calm, but I could see the crazed fear in his eyes as he looked deep. I knew what was coming next. He was going to push his mind into mine to dig to the truth of the matter. My lies would be for nothing. Well, not nothing. I was certainly going to be punished worse for trying to hide the truth. I steeled my nerves. I knew the possible consequences of my actions, and I wasn't going to back away from them just under the threat of pain and death.

Not yet, anyway.

Finally, Vis looked away, pushing me back down onto the cot with a low growl of frustration. He didn't say anything, and again, left me with more questions than answers as he locked the door behind him.

I took a few seconds to calm myself down and to let my hands stop shaking before I reached into my pocket and withdrew the ring. I rubbed at the bronze surface in jerky motions.

"What happened?" Aliana asked, popping into reality out of thin air, as usual. Annoyingly, I was starting to get used to it, though there was still a bile taste in the back of my mouth when she did.

"Vis was asking me questions about what happened that night," I said softly, gripping my hands together. I had been afraid, and as the adrenaline of looking into a future of pain and death faded, there were a variety of signs. Hands sweating and shaking, a sick feeling in my stomach. I gritted my teeth.

"The night we met?" Aliana asked.

I nodded. "I told him more or less what happened, leaving out some crucial details about how I was caught and how I met a djinn. Avoiding anything about how much you helped me was pretty much the idea. I'm not sure if he believed me."

"Well, there are always ways to find out," Aliana said with a small smile. She took me by the hand, guiding me over to the far wall and placed her free hand on it, closing her eyes. There was a warbling sound in my ear for a moment before the sound of Vis' voice could be heard.

"I don't know what to do with him," Vis was saying. "I thought killing his parents might help with bringing the power I know to be in him out to the surface, but nothing. It's like he's actively hiding it from me. I've never seen the like."

"You could always send him to the tower," said a second voice, which sounded like Pollock's. "They know how to handle the difficult cases."

"I am considering it," Vis admitted. "I don't know what else to do with him. Either selling him off to the Tower, or maybe even just killing him. I need to clear any association to what happened. With all the deaths starting to pop up, the farther I am from all this, the better."

"Stop," I said, softly, closing my eyes. "Just stop."

Aliana pulled her hand away from the wall. I shut my eyes, trying to process everything that had just been revealed. Vis had killed my parents, and now wasn't going to bother with keeping me around anymore either. The fact that I had felt any kind of loyalty to the man was making me feel sicker than any trip through a portal.

"What do you want to do?" Aliana asked in a gentle voice.

"Just get me the fuck out of here," I said, trying to keep any sign of emotion from my voice. She nodded, smiling as she squeezed my hand again. I closed my eyes, feeling that tug and twist, dragging my body through like I was in a whirlpool, twisting me around until we dropped down hard on a solid surface. As I looked around, I realized we hadn't actually moved too far away. We were on top of the manor, with a clear view of the rest of the moonlight-bathed countryside.

I had no eye for the beauty of it, I realized, dropping onto the roof and pulling my knees up to my chest.

"You couldn't have gotten us further away?" I asked, looking at Aliana as she dropped to a spot next to me.

"Sorry," Aliana said, sounding genuinely apologetic. "But there is a limit to even my powers. Creating portals through which two can travel is a heavy drain. I will be able to get us further away in a moment. I just need some rest."

I nodded, not really in the mood to talk. Besides the fact that my head was once again aching, it seemed like there was so much to say, but I wanted to be angry. As much as I wanted to lash out at something, I didn't want her to be the target. Not only did I fully expect to be the loser if that happened, but none of this was her fault. All of it was on me and my trusting nature, accepting that Vis had taken me in out of the kindness of his heart after I had been recently orphaned. And the fact that he'd done it because he thought there was some kind of power inside me and not because he felt any kind of guilt over what he'd done just made it worse somehow. I wasn't sure why, but it did.

I looked at Aliana. It seemed like she was in a similarly low mood. I reached over to gently rub her shoulder, squeezing and stroking slowly. She smiled, dropping her head to press her cheek onto my hand.

"I'm sorry for reacting that way about how you handled Kruger and his goons," I said softly. "You saved my life, and all I offered in return was unwarranted judgement. You did what you had to do, and saved my life in the bargain. It was unfair of me. I shouldn't have acted that way."

"You reacted rather better than most in similar situations, I imagine." She pressed her lips to my hand. "All is forgiven, Grant, I assure you."

I opened my mouth to reply but was cut off by the sound of horses galloping into the courtyard below. I drew as close to the edge of the flat roof as I could without skylining myself, looking down to see three men in the telltale Lancer armor riding up to the door. They didn't wait for any servants to arrive, simply climbed down. One was wearing the long, red cloak that indicated he was a high-ranking official.

"What's happening?" I asked, turning to Aliana. I could see she already had her hand on the roof, then heard their voices. "The temporal scars they leave behind when creating portals are difficult to miss, as are the spikes in power when they make them. There is no other explanation. Leave your men here, just in case, but I want this message delivered to the Official right now."

"As you wish, my lord," the Lancer replied.

Aliana pulled us away from the conversation. For the first time since I'd met her, she looked rather terrified.

"Fuck," she spat. "Shit."

"What's the matter? Hey!" I shouted when she didn't answer, just gripped my wrist. We were instantly twisted and twirling through one of her portals again. The pain in my head was only getting worse. When we pulled free from the portal, I couldn't make anything out as the pain worsened to the point that my eyes were clouded with inadvertent tears.

I brushed them away roughly and shook my head to clear it before looking around. We were in what looked like a cave. The mouth opened up to a forest —the forest, unless I missed my guess—and... well, I couldn't make anything out from the back. The ground was firm, though, and while I could hear the sound of trickling water, I saw no evidence of where it was coming from.

I turned to Aliana, who wasn't on her feet as I'd imagined. She was looking at the wall opposite her with a haunted expression on her face, like she couldn't believe what had just happened.

I had questions, but I assumed that now was not the time. We could figure the details out later.

I dropped next to her, draping my arm around her shoulders and drawing her close. The feeling of her wings pressing into my arm was a little unsettling, but I could move past it. I stroked her hair tenderly as I pulled her closer. She smiled, leaning into me. One of her hands moved around my back, but instead of pulling me closer in turn, she slipped it into the pocket that I still had her ring in. She pulled it out, drawing it back up to her eye as she pulled the orb out as well. I had absolutely no idea where from.

She was staring deeply into the orb as her fingers rubbed incessantly at the ring as we cuddled close together. I couldn't see anything changing in the orb myself, but she clearly did, as after almost a half hour, she turned and looked up at me.

"It's high time for you to be the rogue mage you were always meant to be, Grant," she whispered, handing me the ring back.

"What is that supposed to mean?" I asked with a small, confused smile.

"You'll see," she whispered, craning up to press a light kiss on my cheek before settling in for the night.

❧ 10 ❧

I shouldn't have felt as tired as I did. It had been a nice long sleep, deep and without any dreams that I could remember. I should have woken up refreshed, or at least less tired, anyway. I honestly couldn't remember the last time I'd actually woken up refreshed, no matter how long or pleasant a night of sleep I'd had.

But the lack of shutters in the cave slowly brought me to consciousness by letting the sun right into my eyes. After coming out of the deeper sleep, I found myself unable to plunge back in as sleeping on a hard rock made for an ache in my lower back that plagued me until I eventually groaned and pushed myself over, blinking angrily at the sun that was slowly starting to rise.

On the bright side, the damned headache was gone. I took a small comfort in that, at least.

I pushed myself to my feet, groaning softly as I stretched. It had been a long couple of days, I supposed, so it was no surprise that I was more tired than usual. Besides, all the magic that was being forced on me had to be taking some kind of toll, though the actual effects were a bit more difficult to discern.

I looked down at my clothes, realizing that I hadn't changed them since the day before, when I'd been sweating, and had blood soak in. I shook my head, looking around and realizing for the first time that I was alone in the cave.

Where had Aliana disappeared to?

One problem at a time, I mused, moving out of the cave, blinking and yawning. There was the sound of running water nearby. Maybe it was deep enough to fully submerge myself. If not, a quick wash would have to suffice. I moved through the woods toward the sound, surprised as it intensified. Then I realized I was approaching a small waterfall.

I eventually found myself near a couple of deep pools. They were well concealed by bushes and trees which were all fed by a slow-running waterfall. It was a beautiful little nook in the woods, I realized as I smiled and turned my head this way and that, inspecting my surroundings with a great deal of appreciation.

There was a good deal more appreciation when I saw Aliana in one of the pools. Well, she was actually closer to the waterfall, standing on a rock and letting the water flow over her very, very naked body. I couldn't take my eyes away from it caressing her flesh, the sunlight reflecting and glinting on her wet breasts.

My appreciation increased for a moment until I realized that, under the din of the falling water, she wouldn't have been able to hear me approaching and was probably not aware that I was watching her.

That thought was shattered to pieces as she turned to me, smiling sweetly and indicating for me to join her in the water.

For some reason, I shook my head. I wasn't sure why, but it made her laugh as she waded back out into the water, coming over to me. I suddenly realized that having her come closer might not be the best idea. Not for my dignity, anyway. She seemed like the type to point out and tease about the fact that my trousers were in the process of tenting. I quickly dropped to a seat on one of the nearby rocks, trying to cover the visible effects before she made her way out the water.

Amazingly, she seemed even less interested in covering herself as she stepped out and walked over to me. She eyed me curiously, as if wondering for a moment why I'd taken a seat. As she moved closer, her firm breasts glistening in the just-risen sunlight, she could see why.

I misjudged, thinking she would crack a joke about it, since a smile was all that was offered as she moved closer to me.

"What?" I asked as she came nearer, conflicted about whether I wanted her to approach or give me some space.

"My clothes are behind that log," she said with a grin. "Though I would suggest that you take a bath yourself. The water feels amazing."

I nodded, moving to the side but not getting up as she moved around me to reach her clothes. I noticed for the first time that there was a pair of bracelets on her arms. They looked oddly familiar, but I couldn't really place them. I doubted I'd seen them before.

Then again, there was a lot of blood that wasn't going to my brain at the moment, so I would have to readdress the issue once I was finished with my bath.

Yes. A bath. That was what I was going to do, I thought as she moved away, slowly putting her clothes on. Amazingly, they didn't do much for my reaction, so I quickly stripped bare once she was out of sight, moving over to the water.

It was nice, and more importantly it was icy,

causing me to splutter and shiver, all signs of my arousal disappearing as I slipped into the water.

A few minutes later, properly controlled, I managed to clean some of the blood, dirt, and grime from my clothes, and took up the new set as the first was laid out to dry in the sun. I doubted that clean clothes would be something I could rely on for a while, since it was very apparent that we weren't going anywhere near civilization anytime soon, and yet I found myself wanting to cling to at least some kind of practice that showed we weren't wild things.

When I got back to the cave, after only a few minutes lost in the woods, I started to wonder just where we were. The cave was solid rock, which meant we had to be close to the mountains somehow, and yet we were far enough away not to see them. Somewhere at the foot. The mind-wringing fact that somehow Aliana had managed the feat of opening a portal this far away from where we'd been would have to be put aside in light of the fact that we were hundreds of miles away from anything I had relied on for survival over my entire life. I didn't know how to hunt or gather food. I had no idea how to set up a camp, or how to live out here. Sure, we needed to be far away from where the Lancers were, but dying out in the woods wouldn't be a better fate than dying in some dungeon. Well, for me, anyway. I couldn't imagine what they would subject Aliana to if the Emperor got his hands on her.

Then again, she could take care of herself, I mused as I slipped into the cave, looking around, trying to make out just how close to the mountains we were.

"Hey," I heard a voice from behind me.

"You'd think I would be used to you trying to startle me," I said, trying to recover before she noticed.

"I'll continue to do so until it is no longer fun," Aliana said with a small smile as she came around to face me.

"Where are we?" I asked.

"Far enough away from your home that it is unlikely our troubles will follow us," she said. "I brought us here so that you might be able to focus on your training instead of the horde of thoughts that cloud your mind."

"Oh gods, not this again," I groaned, shaking my head. "What will it take to convince you people that I have no fucking power? Do you want me to explain it to you through interpretive dance or something?"

Aliana grinned. "As enjoyable as that might be, I have seen that spark in you. You wouldn't have been able to use that parchment otherwise. There is something in you that keeps it from being displayed to others. It shows an inner nature you want to keep hidden. A roguishness, if you will."

"What is that supposed to mean?" I asked as she guided me out into the forest again.

"The nature of the rogue is to be elusive, a slippery bastard that will not be tamed, no matter what those about him would define as honorable or necessary," she said with a small smile. "I've seen it before, but never quite as independent as yours."

"Is that a compliment?" I asked with a chuckle.

"Not really," she said with a shrug, not sharing my amusement. "Rogues are almost impossible to handle, very difficult to manipulate. It's only possible if you find them young and mold them to one's ways, as Vis did to you. But no matter what he tried, there was always a part of you that refused to submit. Even as you accepted and trusted the man, you found yourself keeping things from him, a part of your mind always stubbornly resisting his instruction."

"So, when you called me a rogue mage last night, that had nothing to do with whatever powers you think I possess?" I mused. I felt stupid for asking these questions, but I was completely out of my depth. I wanted to believe she was right. Over the years I had come to terms with the fact that I would never be able to master magic, but that had never faded the fact that I wanted it for myself.

"Exactly," she said as we came to a stop near the waterfall we had both just come from. She circled around in front of me. Despite the beauty of the surroundings, with the sun filtering through the trees to illuminate everything in a wistful and fantastical presence, all I could really see was the woman in front of me.

I smiled as this time I failed to mentally correct myself. Appearance did not make the man, or the woman, in this case. Horns and wings and odd colors didn't take away from the fact that she was more woman than anyone that I'd ever met. *Not in a sexual way,* I thought. Well, not only in a sexual way. There was no denying that kind of interest in her.

My thoughts were brought to an abrupt halt as she stepped closer, placing her hands on my cheeks.

"There you go again," she whispered. "Always lost in a tangle of your own thoughts and feelings. Stay with me, just this once. Stay in the moment."

I nodded. "I'll try."

She smiled, tilting her head as she watched me. "Now close your eyes and let nothing touch your mind. Let no thought cloud it."

I did as she told me. I wasn't sure what she meant by letting nothing touch my mind. I'd never been able to keep my mind still. There were more than a few teachers that had used similar wording to try and instruct me, but never had I wanted to try as hard as I did now.

"You're still doing it," she whispered, her fingers

moving up to gently rub my temples. "Empty your mind. Let it focus on just one thing."

There was only one thing on my mind right now, but at the moment, that one thing was heavily conflicted. I wanted to reach out and touch her like she was touching me, but I just couldn't do it. I couldn't bring myself to do it.

As I reached the peak of my floundering, she leaned in and pressed her lips gently to mine. For a second, all the conflict disappeared. The softness of her lips was distracting enough that I found my mind going blank, as instructed. There was nothing in my thoughts to tear me away other than what was happening in the moment.

There was another sensation as well. It reminded me, in a way, of how Vis had pushed himself into my mind. The same sensation of shared consciousness was there, but without the torturous pain that the man had needed. Or maybe wanted, I was never sure.

And for a moment, I saw what she was talking about. Feeling my mind expand from beyond the limitations of the body that housed it. Reaching out, like an animal breaking from a long confinement in a cage. Unsure, and more than a little uncoordinated, but free and reaching out for more.

The moment passed, however. I felt her mind still with mine, and there was a moment of curiosity as she reached deeper, trying to touch on something that I'd kept hidden for so long. I wanted to let her, but before she could, the horror of what she might see and what she might think of me if she saw it woke something else in me. Something angry and primal.

Before I knew what I was doing, I pushed her away roughly.

"You were so close," Aliana said softly.

"You had no right to see that," I replied, taking a few steps away.

"Why not?" she asked.

"What I feel about Vis killing my parents is between me and him. It's not... I can't. You don't understand."

"Believe me, Grant, I know a thing or two about wanting revenge. I've even taken it on occasion."

"You don't know anything about me, do you understand that?" I pulled away from her, trying to put some distance between us. She reached out to grab my hand, stopping me, and a sudden and very painful fire rushed through my body. I saw red, and in an instant, all the pain and hatred I'd cultivated for so long about what had happened lashed out. I spun, throwing a wild punch at her face.

It hit nothing but air. I felt her hands roll over my arm, dragging me deeper into the inertia of the punch, which pulled me over her hip to hit the ground on my back. Hard.

A root jutting out of the ground dug deep into my

back, knocking the breath out of my body. For a moment, I was confused about why I was suddenly seeing the sky, blue with tufts of white, when I had been facing Aliana only a moment before.

The rage faded and I realized that I'd just tried to punch the one person who was still on my side in all of this. I looked up at Aliana, who was staring down at me, her expression unreadable.

I groaned, pulling away from the root and rubbing the spot where it felt like it had indented my ribs.

"You forgot that I was more than capable of handing out pain and death to six mercenaries without breaking a sweat there, didn't you?" she asked, an amused look touching her face as I managed to pull myself up to sit against a tree.

I was still finding it hard to breathe, so I just nodded, trying to rub the sore spot in my back and groaning.

"I'm sorry," she said with a small smile, dropping to a squat next to me.

"Don't be," I muttered, still in pain but not wanting to be a baby about it. "I was being unreasonable and stupid."

"Well, yes," she agreed with a small smile. "But all things considered, I think you've earned yourself some unreasonable and stupid moments."

I looked over at her, almost amazed that she was willing to throw off being attacked so easily. Then again, I supposed that if I'd ever really posed any real threat to her, she might have felt differently. I still felt ashamed, though, and it only got worse with each second that passed.

"Look," she said, stroking my cheek with the back of her hand. "If you want to take revenge on someone like Vis, you're going to have to be better at this. Attacking in anger never ends well. You've had some training, I know, but you completely forgot about it in that moment as you prepared to strike. Vis isn't that powerful, but he is powerful enough to beat you right now. If you let me, I can prepare you for that, train you in both mind and in body."

I nodded. "Wait, you approve of this?"

"Like I said, I've taken my fair share of revenge before," she said with a small, cheeky smile. "And I can tell you from experience that if you wish to survive the attempt, you have to approach it with reason and caution. As we kissed, I could feel that you reached out and used your talent. It drew back when you did, but it was there. Now that you know you have the talent for it, all you have to do is emulate the state of mind you were in when you did."

"Arousal?" I asked. That was the state of mind I was in, to be honest.

She chuckled. "Something like that. Who knows? Maybe one day, with practice, I won't even have to be kissing you to bring results."

I opened my mouth, trying to figure out what she meant by that, but she quickly rose and offered me her hand. I was feeling better although there was going to be a bruise on my back, so I took her hand and let her pull me to my feet.

Once I was up, she kept hold of my hand and forced me to look her in the eye.

"Whatever feelings you might have about your parents' death, they won't be resolved by avenging them," she said, looking me firmly in the eye as she spoke.

"I thought you said you approved?" I asked.

"It probably can't hurt," she said with a shrug. "But the point remains. You've learned over the years to wall these kinds of emotions off from yourself, but you need to understand that you're walled in there with them. So long as you put off that personal resolution, there will always be a part of your potential locked away, too."

I opened my mouth to reply, but she stopped me, placing a finger on my lips.

"I don't mean that you should resolve them now," she whispered, stepping closer. "But you will have to, one day. You may not trust me, but know that I want to help you in every way I can."

I ground my teeth, fighting back the surge I could feel welling from my gut. I remembered what it had felt like to be truly alone in the world when my parents died, and, in order to survive, had put those emotions aside. They were painful and put me in a destructive mood each time, so I'd gotten quite talented at keeping them below the surface.

If there was no need to address them now, then I wouldn't, I thought, forcing a smile to my lips.

"Fair enough," I lied. "Now... What was that you said about training me in both mind and body?"

❧ 11 ❧

I blinked the sweat away from my eyes. It proved of little use as my eyes ended up stinging anyway, but I ignored the pain. More an annoyance, really, but at this point, distractions could prove a good deal more painful. I blinked again.

It made no difference. I ground my teeth, gripping the practice stick in my hand tighter as I darted forward.

Aliana smiled, tracking my movements and taking a few steps backward as I feinted to the right, spinning on my heel and coming back around to the left, my 'blade' arcing for her neck. She swayed away from the strike, waiting as it sailed harmlessly past her neck before she aimed a strike at my face with her practice weapon.

I dodged as well, leaning backward to avoid the

cut. I moved a few steps backward, around and to her left, aiming a strike at her flank that she wasn't ready for when my foot caught on a rock. I grunted, tripping and falling hard on my face but not before tapping lightly at her exposed back.

"Well that was embarrassing," she said with a grin, placing her stick on my neck before I could recover. "Almost as embarrassing as that...what do you call it? Beard?"

I scratched at the stubble that had started to grow over the past two weeks or so. It wasn't quite a beard, but it would be in another month or so if left untended. I wasn't overly pleased with it. It looked scruffy and undignified and itched incessantly.

Lacking any tools to shave it, though, I was forced to keep it in place for the moment.

"You're one to talk about questionable choices," I said, pushing myself smoothly to my feet in a single motion, keeping my 'sword' in hand and pointing it at her hair, "with those ridiculous bangs. And how is it that over the two weeks we've spent here, my hair and 'beard' have grown unruly, while yours remains the same, laughable though it may be?"

She reached up to stroke her hair in an instinctive motion, opening her mouth in mock offense. "My hair was considered quite fashionable in my time. And it has never grown. One of the benefits of being what I am is never having to worry about that sort of thing."

"Yes, it was fashionable... what, fifty years ago?" I asked, grinning. "Maybe more?"

"Oh-ho!" she exclaimed, twirling her weapon around. "That's quite a sharp wit you have there. Have you been honing it instead of your fighting skills?"

"What are you talking about?" I asked, moving into a ready stance. "I had you in that last bout."

"Oh please," she replied with a laugh. "You sacrificed your footing and balance for a light tap to my back. That can hardly be considered a victory."

I grinned and would have continued if she didn't move forward again at a blinding speed. I was almost used to seeing her move like that by this point. Fourteen days of practicing to better my skills with magic and combat. Each day brought new challenges, though as a rule, my mornings were spent trying to get a full grasp on my magical talents while the afternoons were spent learning how to fight. She encouraged me to use my magical talents while fighting as well—I knew she did the same, now—and while I still needed practice, much more had been acquired over these past fourteen days than in my entire time at Vis' manor.

I ground my teeth. Just thinking of the man was

enough to boil my blood, but I forced myself to focus on the task at hand.

Too late, I mused as she slipped underneath my attack and hammered her stick into the back of my knee. A shot of pain went up my leg as I was forced down to one knee before she hammered her fist into my jaw, dropping me to the ground. The blow left me sprawled on my back, rubbing where she'd punched.

"On your back, legs spread... isn't that supposed to be my place?" she asked, her head tilting slightly sideways as she swept her gaze over me, grinning. She offered her hand to help me back to my feet.

"Shut up," I grumbled in response, taking her hand, letting her help me back up to my feet.

"Never make fun of my hair again," she replied.

"Noted," I said with a cheeky grin, letting her realize that I would never make such a promise, but would only avoid actually doing it until I was confident enough in my skills that she wouldn't be able to retaliate if I did.

A few more hours passed as we moved on from the practicing sessions to going through different forms of combat, from evasive to power to defensive. I could feel my muscles burning by the end of it, but unlike all those times I'd felt the same way back at Vis' manor, I felt like I was walking away having learned something of value, something that would help come the next time I was placed in front of a table and told to move an apple with my mind.

I was able to move more than apples now, though it was still difficult to keep a grip on the talent. Aliana said it had more to do with my personality than the actual talent. It was an extension of myself that I'd never really controlled, so anything I was on the inside, was reflected in my power.

Which meant that deep inside, I was an annoying, stubborn, horny creature. Good to know.

As the sun set, Aliana moved away to find us something to eat. I made my way over to the waterfall that we used for fresh water as well as to clean ourselves. I pulled my clothes off and slipped under the falling water. Just water and nothing else to clean oneself with had its difficulties, which meant that we were slowly becoming more and more like forest creatures. Well, me, anyway. Aliana somehow managed to look just as good as she had when we'd first arrived. It was distracting, but she said that my being distracted meant that my mind wasn't doing its thing of overworking itself, which allowed me to be able to more easily focus on reaching in.

And she had been right. I was learning to control my power even without having her nearby to keep my mind focused, but it was easier with her around. I was even starting to get used to being slightly aroused almost constantly. It was interesting how that effect didn't fade over time, for some reason.

I washed the sweat from my body and moved back to reclaim my clothes only to find them missing. I knew I'd left them hanging over a rock, picked precisely for the purpose that it was still in the fading sunlight and still warm to the touch. I looked around, raising an eyebrow as I saw tracks leading back to the cave. There was only one person out here, which meant that for some reason known only to her, Aliana had taken my clothes.

She had been acting oddly. She'd told me that she would respect my wishes about not wanting to sleep with someone who was tied to me as she was, but that didn't keep her from being rather affectionate with her hands and lips, making sure the arousal never really left.

So, sadly, I could in all honesty say that her stealing my clothes as a prank wasn't really out of character for her.

I made my way back to the cave, not bothering to cover myself on the way there. Who was going to peep on me all the way out here who hadn't already seen everything there was to see? It was actually rather liberating to live like this. I wasn't going to pretend I didn't miss having clean clothes to wear, or a hot bath and a razor-sharp blade to shave with. Aliana had refused to loan me her knives for the task.

As I approached the cave, Aliana stepped out, openly admiring the view.

"Very funny," I said, crossing my arms over my bare chest. "Stealing my clothes as I clean myself. Hilarious. Now give them back."

"I've given them a wash," she said with a smile. "And they needed them."

"I need them too," I pointed out.

"Not for the moment," she said, coming over to me and taking my arm, tugging me inside with her. I followed her deeper into the cave. Some effort had been put into making it more livable. Soft pine needles had been scrounged up from outside and wrapped to make improvised blankets, and a section of the cave had been marked off for a fire as well as what food and supplies we either had with us or were able to acquire this far out in civilization. I wasn't sure if I could call it living, as such, but it was certainly a decent way to survive while we were out here training.

But something had changed. I wasn't sure how she'd done it in such a short time, but most of the back of the cave had been arranged differently. There had always been the sound of water moving, but she had somehow found it, using it to fill a small pool, deep enough for me to submerge myself in, just barely.

"Get in," she said with a smile. "It's quite warm."

"How?" I asked. Neither of us liked chopping wood for a fire. She couldn't have taken the time to get enough to heat up that much water.

"As much as I want to say that I put a lot of work or magic into it," Aliana said with a small smile as she nudged me closer to it, "I must admit that the mountain did the work for me."

"What?" I asked, moving closer. As my feet touched the water, I realized she was right. The water was rather warm.

"The heat from the mountain warms the water beneath it," she said, nudging me forward until I was thigh deep in the impossibly warm water. I had no idea how a mountain was supposed to warm water, but at the moment, I didn't really care as I dropped, sinking my body into it with a loud, audible groan.

"Fuck, that's good," I sighed as everything from my neck down was submerged in the clear water. For the moment I almost completely forgot there was someone else in the cave with me. That was, until I felt the water shifting ever so slightly, indicating that Aliana was joining me in the pool. I opened my eyes and stared for a moment as I realized she had gotten rid of her clothes too. She knelt next to me, the water rising up to her stomach, almost to her breasts as she settled down next to me.

I opened my mouth to speak, but she put her finger on my lips. She had a habit of doing that, knowing that it was a lot more diplomatic and distracting than just telling me to shut up. Her hands moved into the water and toward my body but stopped just shy of touching my bare skin.

Even without our skin touching, I could feel something reaching through the water as she closed her eyes. Something pressing gently against my skin as she stroked up and down over my chest, neck and back. As her hands moved, I saw them dislodging the dirt, sweat and grime that had built up over the past two weeks, washing it away. I could feel myself relaxing with each stroke. The stresses, the pain from our training, my worry over what would come next was being pushed into the back of my mind. There was magic involved, but it was far too complex for me to have any idea how it worked.

I stiffened when I felt her hands moving down lower than my stomach, reaching a particular bit of me that wasn't relaxed at all.

"I think I can clean that for myself, thanks," I said, my voice throatier than intended.

"I don't have to be a mind reader to tell that you want me," she whispered. "And I want you, too. Why can't you just give in?"

"I want it," I admitted through gritted teeth. "Don't think for a second that I don't. I'd have to be an idiot otherwise. I would have said blind but even a blind man—"

"Grant," she chided softly. "Focus."

"Right." I looked up at her. "Bound to me like this, I just can't... I can't put it out of my mind that I'd be making you do something you don't want. You say you want it, but I have no idea what you'd want if you were free of... whatever this fucking ring does." I raised my hand. I'd taken to wearing it since I didn't want to lose it.

"Then free me, help me find my sisters, and find out," she whispered.

I still had both of her hands in mine. I raised them to my eye level, inspecting them closely before looking into her eyes.

"I want you to be free," I whispered softly, intensely. "But I don't know how to do it."

She didn't answer me. Her eyes locked with mine for a long moment as she leaned in, leaving her hands in my grasp as she pressed her lips to mine. It was a hungry kiss at first. She leaned into me hard enough to almost completely submerge me in the water, but after a few seconds, the intensity faded, leaving us gently pressed together before she pulled away.

My eyes remained closed for a few long moments, basking in the aftereffects of the kiss. I suddenly realized I'd been forgetting to breathe and inhaled before opening my eyes again. They were greeted with the sight of her hands still in mine. There was something different about her, but it took me longer than I would have liked to realize what it was.

"Your bracelets. They're gone."

"That was all it took," she said with broad grin. "It's like I keep telling you. Focus and will is much more important than technique. A lesson that applies to a great many other fields than just magic, you should know."

"Noted," I said with a nod. I looked down at the ring I wore on my finger. I barely even noticed it anymore. "Does that mean you can't just slip back into the ring if we need to hide?" I asked, attempting to joke. It wasn't great, by the shaking of Aliana's head as she leaned in to kiss me again. This time I pushed back, moaning softly into the kiss.

"Now do you believe that I want you, with no ulterior motives?" she asked, with a small smile.

"Well, I could always use some more convincing," I said as I looked up at her.

"Say no more," she murmured, pressing light kisses to my cheek, trailing down my jawline, over my throat and shoulder as her hands moved further in advance. I was still unbearably aroused, and the whole two weeks spent with her hadn't helped with that. I was aching for release.

And she could feel it. From the shaft that throbbed in her hands to the soft gasps coming from my lips as she pressed her body to mine, her kisses trailing down my chest, over my stomach and finally, as she pulled me a bit further out of the water so that I was fully exposed, she pressed a light kiss to the thick head.

"Oh gods," I whispered, my head falling back as I felt her tongue darting out to toy with it, running down the underside of the shaft before climbing back up, her hands alternating between stroking me slowly and caressing my balls underneath. It was difficult to describe the number of sensations rushing up and down my spine at the moment. Besides, I was supposed to keep my mind from interfering with what I was feeling.

I pulled myself up, suddenly wanting to watch as she slipped my cock into her mouth, teasing at it with her lips first before sloppily sucking it in. She pressed it to her right cheek then the left before bobbing her head a few times, moaning loudly and letting me feel the vibrations from her throat, sending shivers up my spine from the way they shuddered around my shaft.

She reached up, grabbing one of my hands and pulling it down to tangle with her long hair as she started bobbing her head over me. My hands curled around her horns, toying with them curiously before threading through her locks. She took the second hand too, but this one she guided down to her breasts. She had to know I wanted to touch them, from the amount of time I'd spent pretending not to stare. I moved with her, careful to keep my hips from thrusting as she fed herself more and more of my thick shaft.

My fingers gripped her breast at first, almost disbelieving how firm and yet soft it was. It was heavy in my palm, the nipple hardening as I rubbed my calloused hand over it. I kneaded the soft flesh for a few moments, closing my eyes and letting the fullness of the sensations wash over me. From the way her head felt against my hand, enthusiastically moving up and down over my cock, to the weight and delicious softness of her breast. I was still laying back on the hard rock, with the warm water lapping gently over my suddenly very hot skin, all mixing together to create something. I couldn't tell what it was, but I knew I wanted more of it.

She moaned, smiling and looking up at me in approval as she felt my hips starting to move in time with her mouth, my fingers gripping the back of her head tighter, toying with her horns as the other hand started toying gently with the nipple between my forefinger and thumb, squeezing, tugging. Her moans of encouragement and pleasure only drove me further.

My hips thrust harder, and my grip tightened to the point where I stole the control from her, feeding her my cock in rough thrusts over and over again as she gripped my hips, then my ass, nails digging into my skin, wanting me to thrust harder before I felt shots of pleasure rushing through my body, focusing on where her mouth and hands were as I bucked hard, feeling my warm seed soak into her mouth. She moaned encouragingly, taking hold of the shaft with her right hand and coaxing more and more until I dropped back, feeling the shallow water sloshing around me.

She remained where she was, poised between my thighs, the head of my cock in her mouth as she kept milking me for every last drop. Over the past two weeks, enough had accumulated.

Finally, she pulled away with a sigh, swallowing and smacking her lips.

"You taste good." She pressed light kisses up my body as she dragged herself over it until she was laying over me, breasts pressed firmly into my chest as she kissed me tenderly.

I hesitated for a moment as I realized where her lips had been before, and the fact that there was a new taste in her mouth which I could only assume was from me. It was interesting, but not in a bad way. After coming to terms with the thought, I leaned into the kiss a bit more before pulling back.

"I'm sorry if I handled you roughly toward the end, there," I whispered.

"I can't speak for all women," she replied. "But I

can say for myself that I rather enjoy being roughly handled. Especially when the ending is that satisfying." She pushed herself up and placed a kiss on the tip of my nose. "Although if you'd like to make up for it, I think I know a couple of things you could do."

"Oh?" I asked, watching as she rolled off of me. There was a moment of regret as I missed the feel of her almost inhumanly hot skin pressed against mine. She didn't move too far away, though. In fact, she just rolled onto her back right next to me and was quick to pull me with her as I half-lay over her, kissing her lips tenderly.

"What did you have in mind?" I asked, letting the words out each time my lips parted from moving down her neck and shoulders.

"Mmm." She didn't reply for a moment, just closing her eyes and enjoying herself. "Well, I thought about something rather similar to what I was just doing."

She paused as I moved down, my hand playing with one of her breasts while my mouth latched onto the nipple of the other. Sucking, kissing, licking and teasing playfully as I could feel her growing a bit more aroused.

"Come," she whispered, a sense of urgency entering her voice as she spread her legs wider. I took that as an invitation, slipping between them as I continued kissing her skin. She trailed the fingers of one hand down her side, guiding me down before taking hold of my hand again. She wasn't afraid to let me know what she wanted, I realized with a small smile, still feeling the warm water lapping around us in response to our movements. It was a soothing, rhythmic sensation that I rather enjoyed.

"Here," she said, pushing my hand down between her legs where I found a thin strip of hair leading my eyes down to her pussy. I could see she was already wet as she pressed her hand to it. She guided my fingers to part the lips, rubbing my thumb on the small nub that presented itself there.

Not needing any more indication, I dropped my head, following her leading hand as I used my hands to keep her lips parted and applied the rough wetness of my tongue to the nub. Her reaction was almost instant. Her back arched and a low moan escaped her lips as her hands gripped the back of my head more insistently. I took that as a good sign, working my tongue over her clit some more as my hands started to explore. I could feel her thighs wrapping around the sides of my head and squeezing gently, but I really didn't mind.

I dipped my head further, finding the source of the delicious wetness. I could hear her moaning insistently, her hands almost confused about what she wanted as I pushed my tongue inside her, moaning in response as she gasped.

Out of pure instinct, I reached up, feeling the softness of her breast pressed into my hand again as she pulled me back up to pay homage to the delicious nub. As my tongue slipped out of her, my fingers took their position. First only one, and then two, slowly starting to pump into her wet pussy.

"Oh fuck, Grant," she whispered. "Oh yes... that's it... a bit to the lef.... Ooooohhhh..." I could feel her body shaking and shuddering, wings fluttering in excitement and pleasure. I hadn't been sure if she meant my fingers or my tongue, so I moved both, and the results were encouraging. I felt a small bump deep inside her pussy, and the reactions from that seemed to pull more reactions from her. She had lost the ability to say anything that wasn't an elongated vowel, so I simply applied myself to what she'd shown me. Her pussy tightening as I brushed my fingers over that bump in time with my tongue over her clit had her gasping and her hips bucking like mine did when I came, leading me to believe that she was coming too.

Hers lasted longer than mine did though as I felt her cum drench my fingers and mouth. I wanted more. Demanded more, almost, as I kept working, kept sucking and pumping until I felt her bucking and gripping me again. Her hands were pulling at my hair, trying to drag me out from between her thighs, which were sending a different message, pinning me in place. The cave was awash with her moans of pleasure, soft gasps and delicious growls.

Finally, as I pulled away, I heard a soft sound of pleasure shudder from her lips. She dropped against the ground in relief as I finally let up.

"You are a natural at this," she whispered with a small smile, pulling me closer to reward me with a long, delicious kiss. I wondered if she could taste herself on me like I had, but from her moans, she didn't seem to mind either way.

We moved away from the warm water of the pool, seeing that night had fallen outside while we'd been inside the cave enjoying ourselves. We'd spent the nights in two different 'beds,' improvised as they were, but this time she joined me in mine instead. Due to her wings, she had to settle in behind me, but I didn't really mind, and feeling her body wrapping around mine was more comforting than I thought it would be.

It wasn't long before we both drifted off to sleep.

🦎 12 🦎

It had been a while since I'd been back, I thought. Aliana told me that she had been taking daily trips into the city, using her portals to get in and out and that magical field of hers to stay out of sight while trying to keep an eye out for Norel, as well as making sure she knew what Vis and Pollock were up to.

I assumed she could have done it without as much effort by using the orb she'd taken from Kruger's men, but as often as I found her softly cursing at it when she thought I couldn't hear, I assumed she was having troubles with that as well.

I asked why she didn't take me with her to go scouting, and she answered, with painful honesty, that I wasn't ready to return yet. I wasn't sure if she meant to say that I wasn't ready to be in the same room as

Vis again, or that even as quickly as I was advancing with improving on my talents, I just wasn't ready to defend myself should trouble arise.

Either meaning hurt my ego, but it only drove me to work better and harder, keeping up with her instruction and hoping that eventually she would think I was ready, one way or the other.

A few days after we'd been together, I heard the warbling, twisting sound of her creating one of her portals. Or stepping through one. There wasn't much difference between the two, but I could tell it was one she was returning through since I'd seen her leave. More specifically, she'd told me to keep working on my training even while she was gone, before disappearing.

There was a small part of me that was really thankful I wasn't going with her, if only because it meant not having to deal with the awful headaches that came a direct result of them.

I knew that she would know if I'd been training or lazing around while she was gone, so I made sure to run through all the various forms and motions that she'd taught me for about three hours. I'd finished, and since she hadn't returned, I took to meditating. Oddly enough, after that... rather enjoyable bath we'd shared, I'd somehow found it easier to focus, even when she wasn't around. Taking deep breaths, I closed my eyes again, reaching out into the world around me. I could feel the trees moving in the wind, which had picked up as the summer months were starting to wane. There were animals all around us, all seeming to ignore the fact that I was just sitting there, reaching out and exploring. I could feel Aliana too, walking over toward me.

With what control I had over my talent, I took a phantom grip on her top and undid it as she came closer.

"Hey now!" she protested as I opened my eyes, licking my lips at the delicious view she presented me with before she quickly put it back on. "Behave. While you're training, at least."

"I was practicing my phantom grip," I said, keeping a straight face. She laughed, shaking her head as she took her place next to me. I noticed she was carrying a pack over her shoulder.

"What have you got there?" I asked. She never carried packs. I wasn't even sure where she carried her dagger. It just seemed to appear out of thin air when she needed it.

"I managed to steal some food while I was at your former master's manor," she said, pulling the pack open and showing me a couple of loaves of bread, strips of dried meat, apples and cheese. I wasn't sure how, but my mouth was full of water all of a sudden. I normally would have complained about the repast, but after this long of only having fruits, berries, and other treasures offered up by the forest, it looked like a feast worthy of the Emperor himself.

"I brought news too," she said, tapping lightly on my shoulder. "I'll tell you while we eat."

I nodded, eagerly following her back to the cave. She seemed almost as hungry for proper food as I was, and the first five minutes after we returned was spent hungrily digging into the feast she'd brought back. I felt bad for the servants that would be held responsible for food having gone missing, but I could deal with that later. There were more pressing matters at hand right now.

Once we were finished and spent a few minutes laying back and enjoying the gorgeous sunset we could see from inside the cave while taking small sips of the clear water from the waterfall, I turned onto my side to face Aliana.

"You said you had news," I said as I laid next to her. "We were both rather engrossed in the food, but now that we're finished... care to share it with me?"

She turned on her side to face me, placing a light kiss on my lips. I was getting used to having her this close to me. Not so used to it that I wasn't in a near-constant state of arousal, but enough that I knew to look past that.

"Well, I managed to pick up some news from servants in Vis' manor," she said, kissing my cheek as well before leaning back, her wings spreading lazily to catch the wind drifting into the cave.

"I don't suppose they noticed that I was missing at all, the bastards," I said. "Probably already moved on and found a new familiar to replace me."

"You actually could not be more wrong about that," Aliana replied with a chuckle. "You should know that after we disappeared, Vis spent a good deal of time and effort as well as coin to find us again. There was a man called Cyron that he was working for in doing that, and he fears this Cyron so much that when he failed to produce any results, Vis went into hiding as well."

"Cyron?" I asked, tilting my head in thought. The name was familiar to me, but it took me a few seconds to place a face to it. "Oh right. He's another noble, well above Vis in station and power. The two have never been rivals at all, but they seem to have a kind of relationship of love as well as hate, since the two seem to be the only ones who can tolerate each other in the Emperor's court."

"Well, be that as it may, Vis was terrified of the man," Aliana said softly, her hand running idly up my side. "He and Pollock appeared to be under this Cyron's thumb. From what I could tell—and this is something I've heard before, and not from Vis' servants—Pollock and Vis were trying to pry themselves out from under the man's power. Stealing the parchment, which would have led them to me if you hadn't encountered me first, was supposed to be the first step in achieving that. When that failed, they turned on each other, trying to point blame. They failed, and now both are fearing the man's wrath. Odd little humans."

I nodded, although I mused that it wasn't that odd to fear a man like Cyron. Lesser, perhaps, in standing than others in the court, but that was only because he was considered unlikeable by the rest, which made rising in the ranks difficult. Even so, he was more powerful than his station let on.

"Wait," I said. "Pollock knew about what you were. He said djinn specifically, by name. To everyone else I know, the djinn are no more than children's fiction, and yet to him, well, you were real. More importantly, he knew what he was looking for. I don't remember his exact words but..."

"Temporal scars from my portals," Aliana said softly. "And spikes in power that were unique to my kind. What is your point?"

"If Cyron is the one who's behind all this," I said, speaking softly, "he would be the one behind getting that parchment in the first place. Maybe not the one behind stealing it, but if it was what someone might need to find you, that says he was looking for you. For my part, all I did was stumble onto you through sheer luck."

"Magic, and the parchment, actually," Aliana corrected me with a small smile.

"Right," I agreed, not wanting to get into that argument again. "But that would mean that Cyron was looking for you specifically. A man like him wouldn't go looking for something everyone else thinks is a fairy tale unless he had something in mind for you. Something that made Vis and Pollock, politicians and cowards under ordinary circumstances, rise against him and try to stop whatever it was he was planning."

Aliana narrowed her eyes, taking a deep breath as she pondered what I'd just said. Sure, most if not all of it was conjecture, but it fit what had been happening so far.

"If Cyron was looking for me," Aliana said, finally breaking the silence, "what the fuck would he want?"

"You're powerful," I said bluntly. "You have a great deal of magical knowledge and ability. If Cyron had encountered the ring before me, he would have had control over you. Which, I'm still not entirely sure how that works?"

"It's complicated," Aliana replied. It wasn't the first time she'd given me that answer and honestly, I was getting tired of prying.

"Anyway, if he had that amount of control over you..." I paused. It was painful to even think about her being forced into the will of a man as foul as Cyron.

"There's no telling what he would have done," Aliana completed for me, leaning closer to stroke my hair. From the way her wings had fallen still, I realized that thought made her blood run cold, too.

"Cyron, like Vis or Pollock, is an ambitious man," I murmured. "He wouldn't have put his plan entirely on finding something that nobody was really sure existed in the first place. He would have had alternatives."

"You're not thinking what I think you're thinking, are you?" Aliana asked, staring at me.

"We have to find a way to stop him from doing whatever it is he's planning. Which means we have to find out what he wants to do, first."

"I'm hearing a lot of 'we's in that plan of yours," she said in a warning tone. "I still don't think you're ready to go back there."

"We wouldn't be here if you could find out what was happening yourself," I said. "From what I've been able to figure out, you wouldn't be able to get through them and keep your field of... perception alteration intact."

"Excuse you," she said, leaning closer. "I can get in just fine, thank you very much. It's getting out that proves to be the greater difficulty."

"I can help," I whispered, tracing my finger over

her cheek. It still made me smile to feel just how hot her skin was to the touch.

"You're still not ready to go back alone," she said with a small smile.

"Well, that's what you'll be there for, isn't it?" I asked with a small, teasing smile, making her laugh in response. I leaned in to press a light kiss on her lips. She moaned softly, running her fingers through my hair in a way that sent chills down my spine.

"How about your sister? How is she?" I asked after we parted lips.

"I can't ever get close enough to see her in person," Aliana whispered, looking away. "I can still find her through the orb, but I've been having some trouble with it of late. It just goes to show what happens when you put a magical seeing orb in the hands of a dimwit who thinks that it's just a pretty bauble."

"Why can't you get close enough?" I asked. She refused to meet my glance, turning onto her back to stare at the roof of the cave.

"I'm not sure how," she finally replied. "It's been so long. So much has happened since we parted ways. I thought it would be forever the last time we saw each other. It was difficult, and I'm not sure I can face that again."

I turned onto my back as well. These kinds of conversations were easier to hold when the participants weren't looking at each other, I realized with a small smile.

"Not to be disrespectful," I said, keeping my voice low. "But wasn't it you who told me that walling these sorts of things off walls a part of yourself off as well? If you don't address this, it'll just get more and more difficult, until you can't anymore, and you'll end up regretting that missed chance for the rest of your life."

"Using my words against me," Aliana said with a soft chuckle. "Well played, Grant. Well played."

"I thank you," I replied with a grin. "So, it's decided? We head on over to the city. We work together to try and find out what it is that Cyron is up to. And if we find anything of note, we can bring it to Norel. She seems to be in a position to be able to do something about it if the man's plans prove to be devious enough, and we can take advantage of that to get you two together again. What say you?"

She turned over to face me, leaning in to kiss my cheek. "That sounds like a good plan. I'll sleep on it, and let you know."

I wrapped my arms around her shoulder, smoothly avoiding her wings, and pulled her closer as we drifted off to sleep.

❧ 13 ❧

I was getting used to having someone with me in bed. Summer was starting to turn into fall and the nights were getting colder out in the wilds. Having someone to share that cold with, especially in the absence of a real bed or anything in the way of sheets or pillows, made the experience a bit less like survival and a bit more like living. Besides, the fact that her skin was hotter than what one would find with humans was an added boon in that regard.

I woke up before Aliana, the first time that had happened since we got out here. I made my way out, rubbing my eyes, making sure to move as quietly as possible as I stepped out of the cave as nature called. Once finished, I walked down to the waterfall, taking a moment to splash my face with the cool water to help me wake up. As the water stilled once more, I looked into my reflection. There wasn't much about it I liked, I realized. There was a gaunter look about me. The muscles in my shoulders and arms were more defined, but the stubble growing over my cheeks made me look like a wild creature of the forest.

It hadn't yet been a month and I already looked like a man who hadn't seen the light of civilization in decades. I scratched my chin, still scowling at my reflection before turning back around and heading back to the cave. What made it worse was the fact that Aliana literally hadn't changed from the moment we arrived. She was still as mouth-wateringly gorgeous as she had been when we first got here. As delightful as that was for me, I was having difficulties understanding how she could stand to be around me.

When I got back to the cave, I realized Aliana had been up for a little while, setting out what food was left from what she'd stolen the day before. I sat down beside her, next to the fire, taking a bite out of the bread and dried meat and chewing slowly as I watched the flames licking at the last of our wood. One of us would have to go chop more sometime today.

That was assuming, of course, that we were going to be staying around long enough to make use of it.

I looked at her, realizing that she was staring at me as well. Though her gaze was on me, there was an absent look in her eyes that told me that her mind was far, far away. I moved closer close to her as I looked outside.

"What's on your mind?" I asked in a soft voice. I knew what was on her mind, but I didn't want to intrude on what might be a private moment.

She looked over at me, smiling as her mind came back to us. She reached out to gently run her fingers over my cheek. It was a soft touch but sent chills through my body and made me smile back.

"Just thinking over what we were talking about last night," she said quietly. "If we were to find out what Cyron was up to, how would we go about it?"

"We would probably have to get in beyond the outer wards placed on the walls of his mansion," I replied, cocking my head as I tried to remember what the place looked like. I had been there a few times, but I had been isolated in the servant's quarters for the duration, so I didn't know much about the layout. Whenever Vis had sent me off to steal from some-one, he'd always had some plans laid out so I knew where to get in and out once I'd found what he'd wanted.

Just thinking about the man was enough to set my blood boiling, I realized, grinding my teeth. Aliana seemed to read my mind. She reached out to stroke my cheek again, this time on the other side, pulling my attention back to her.

I looked at her, trying to push aside the cloud of red that had descended on me for a moment and forced a smile.

"How do you propose we get there?" I asked after a couple of moments. "Well, I assume we'll being using one of those odd portals of yours, but how do we get past the wards?"

"Would it interest you to know that I can get us inside any location without triggering the wards that protect it, when I know what to prepare for?" Aliana asked, chuckling. "If we find our way inside, we won't need to alert anyone to our whereabouts."

I thought about it. "That's useful, I suppose, but I would guess that if Cyron is concealing something, he'll have made precautions that extend inside the borders of his mansion. No, we have to get close enough to tell when the wards are being reset by his familiars. Maybe we could find a way to forge our entry through their inexperienced hands?"

"Seems simple enough," Aliana said with a smile. Yes, I supposed something that would have given even grandmasters pause would be simple enough. "Do you have anywhere in mind?"

"There's a library connected to his mansion by walls," I replied with a smile. "It's also connected to the Lancer's guardhouse, but they don't make use of it. In fact, it should be rather deserted around this time of year. The men that care for the books are usually off to the mountains to catch sight of the Midnight Sun."

"How do you know about this?" she asked.

"I have an interest in books," I replied. "And in learning. It was always kept limited by Vis, since he had a very simple goal in mind for all his familiars; just enough knowledge to make them useful, but never enough for them to be capable of independent thought."

Aliana looked down. I could see the thoughts churning in her head. I could tell she was having second thoughts about helping me pursue my vengeance, even though she knew it was what had driven me thus far. I could understand why she was thinking that, but it didn't change the fact that I was going to kill the man the next time I saw him. Vengeance in the moment, and a life-time of apologies to make up for it once it was done.

I snapped back to reality. "If we're leaving, we should probably clear any trace of our having stayed here. Wouldn't want us to be tracked down, would we?"

"I guess not," Aliana said softly, leaning back in her seat as we finished what remained of our food stores. It was an interesting feeling to not have to worry about them anymore. So many problems that came with living out here in the wild would be discarded, only to be replaced by the more pressing concerns of survival back in my hometown.

Hopefully, they would come with a razor. The stubble growing on my face itched hellishly.

It was almost midday by the time we were finished covering any trace of our living here. I knew there wasn't much chance of the cave being discovered this deep in the forest, but there was no sense in not being careful.

Aliana joined me by the waterfall after she was finished, smiling and moving closer to me.

"Are you ready?" she asked.

"Yes," I answered, turning to face her.

"I'm going to need to look into your mind to find this library," she said, running her hands up my chest and placing them on my temples. "And maybe, as I do, you can figure out how to do this for yourself through the connection."

I nodded, closing my eyes as I felt her consciousness pressing into mine. It was a two-way connection, I realized. Just as much as she was reaching into my mind, I could see into hers with equal clarity. There were more than a few things hidden away in the deep, dark recesses that I assumed she didn't want me to see, but those that weren't were rather interesting as well. It was nice to know that she was just as aroused by me as I was by her, and even more interesting, that she was having a bit of trouble focusing her mind as she was thinking about the last time we'd been this close to each other.

"Focus," she chided softly, although I wasn't sure if she was talking to me or to herself. I felt her find the image of the library I'd told her about. Once the connection was established, she parted from me, pulling away to create the portal. After a few seconds, she reached out and grabbed my shoulder and I felt the familiar sensation of vertigo rushing through my body as I was pulled, twisting and turning, through whatever it was that opened.

We came out just as quickly as we'd entered, dropping into a small room full of dusty scrolls. The smell of old parchment was all I could focus on for a moment as we recovered from the transportation. I took a breath, fighting back the nausea that was starting to rise in the back of my throat. I leaned back, inhaling slowly as I looked around, trying to come to terms with the fact that we were in a room with actual walls and ceilings again. And a window, I realized, looking up at the only source of light illuminating the room.

I moved over to a couple of the scrolls. We were in the history section of the library, I realized, not something that was visited often even when the place was bustling with activity. Today, it was just as abandoned as the rest of the place.

I found a scroll depicting the massacre at Vizier's

Castle in close detail, and found a seat nearby to dig into it.

"What are you doing?" Aliana asked, watching me.

"Reading," I said, pointing at the scroll. "Or, trying to, anyway. Whomever has the job maintaining these scrolls should lose it."

"Don't you think we have more important things to do at the moment?" she asked.

I looked up at her. "Did I forget to mention? The familiars don't replace the wards until sunset. Cyron is superstitious when it comes to performing the rites while in full view of the sun and the moon. I'm not really sure where that comes from, but it does give us a reliable schedule."

"Oh," Aliana grunted then chuckled. "And you forgot to mention that?"

"Well, I did have some ulterior motives," I said with a grin. "For one thing, I would have been too distracted to train, and knowing you, you would have made me do it anyways. Besides, I was banned from this library for a while so I wanted a chance to be where I could learn while we waited."

"Oh," she grunted again. "So, you manipulated me."

"Masterfully," I said with a grin. "But come on, who wouldn't want to spend a nice afternoon being distracted by some well-written books and stories of the past, as well as those that cover the various magical aspects I'm trying to master?"

"Someone who was around for some of those historical events, or the person who already knows about the various magical aspects you're trying to master," Aliana said a soft voice.

"Oh, right," I said. Sometimes, it was easy to forget that she was at least fifty years older than I. The fact that she was infinitely more powerful did come up more often, which was why I blamed myself entirely for forgetting it. "So, what do you think we should do?"

"Well, you assume I would have had you training all day," she said, plucking the scroll out of my fingers and tossing it to the side as she took its place on my lap, making sure to wiggle her ass into me a bit before draping her arms around my neck. "When we would have had so many other things to occupy the time."

I almost lost track of what she was saying, my thoughts still on the scantily-clad posterior pressing very closely, actually right on top of my cock. For some reason, I was trying to keep from having any kind of reaction she'd be able to notice. I wasn't sure why. It wasn't like she hadn't seen me like that before, and in a lot of cases, she seemed to actually encourage it. Some old habits were hard to get rid of.

It seemed like she could sense my internal strug-gle. Like my arousal, she seemed to be encouraging it, shifting herself over my lap a bit more, like she was trying to get more of a reaction as she leaned in closer. I could feel her breasts pressing into my chest as her lips glided lightly over my jaw. I could hear her saying something but I couldn't quite make it out. Besides, if I leaned back to see her lips, I had little doubt she would follow me and that would leave us in an even more compromising position.

Even so, as she leaned closer, kissing her way up my jaw and taking my earlobe between her teeth, I found that concealing my arousal was impossible. She giggled softly as she felt it pressing into her ass and pushed back harder, sending a surge of sensation rushing through my body as she kept on whispering in my ear.

I caught a flicker of motion as her wings flapped gently, probably out of instinct, as she moved up over me, straddling me as she pressed in closer, her lips still remaining right up next to my ear. She was still whispering, and I still couldn't make it out. Not that I needed to, as the movement of her climbing on top of me had pulled her top down far enough that I could feel her pert, hard nipples rubbing into my chest through my clothes.

"This is certainly one way to pass the time," I said, feeling myself come to full mast and press up against her as she started grinding into me.

She didn't respond verbally, or at least not in any

way I could understand although she continued whispering. I could feel her wrapping her arms around me tighter, pulling me closer as my hands glided up her sides then cupped and squeezed her breasts. Somehow, I had forgotten how delicious they felt, firm yet soft between my fingers. Her words changed to sounds more like moans. I could feel her arousal now, too. Not just from the hardening nipples in my hands, but from the wet heat I could feel between her legs, as she ground against my throbbing erection.

The way her tongue and lips felt against my earlobe reminded me just how her mouth felt against my cock, drawing my imagination to thoughts I'd been having the night before. Not just of her mouth, but her breasts too and the wet pussy I could feel grinding against me. I felt a surge of pleasure rushing through my body as she kept on whispering and grinding.

I pulled back as I suddenly realized what was happening. Runes were starting to rise from her arms, given light and form by what she was saying. She looked me in the eye, grinning as I realized what she was up to, leaning in to press a long, tender kiss to my lips.

"What the hell was that?" I whispered breathlessly. "There are actual magical incantations to get a man hard and...to orgasm?"

"Not as such, no," she replied, still close enough

to me that I could feel her hot breath on my cheek. "Certain words can help any man or woman, of any race really, to indulge them and put them in a state of mind where they could be easily coaxed into that, yes."

I raised an eyebrow. "Sounds like a useful trick. And one that I intend to return the favor on presently."

She grinned. "Well, you still have some sort of puritanical holdback over fucking me, so a woman needs to find what loopholes she can if she's to get some satisfaction, wouldn't you say?"

I grinned, leaning back again in my seat, licking my lips and trying to wrap my mind around what had just happened. I'd always seen magic as something mighty and powerful, used for mighty and powerful things, never to be squandered on something as simple and dirty as getting someone in the mood for sex.

Then again, I recalled how I'd found Vis on that fateful night and realized how stupid I was for clinging to that kind of idealistic nonsense. Whatever it had been made for originally, as long as there were people in the world who put priority on anything, there would be ways to bend any kind of power toward these priorities.

The hours seemed to pass by quickly. Though it

seemed that Aliana had lost interest in further pushing me with her magic after I discovered what she was up to, she still didn't want to budge from her perch atop me. She smiled and moaned softly as I leaned back further, letting her lay her head on my chest. It meant that I had to move a bit to keep her horns from poking at my chin every time I inhaled, but the way she seemed so contented laying on top of me, her wings settling over us like the oddest kind of blanket, I couldn't bear to budge. Considering that she wasn't human, I could never tell if she was asleep or not just from her breathing patterns, but with her eyes closed and the smile on her face, it seemed like she was.

It hit me that while my puritanical views, as she put it, had kept me from fully engaging, she had no such views.

It would have explained why she'd stopped, I supposed. She couldn't have known if I'd come or not, but she could have assumed that since she had, I had too which was why I was the one to stop her.

I really needed to get over whatever it was that was stopping me.

I looked up from watching her sleep on top of me, seeing that the sun was starting to disappear from sight through the window and I nudged Aliana gently. She made no sign that she'd felt it, so I poked her gently in the side. She squeaked loudly, dropping from where she was lying to the ground. I groaned softly as I pushed myself up.

"What was that for?" she asked, looking annoyed.

"Other than finding out if you're ticklish or not?" I asked, pulling myself to my feet and stretching. "The sun is starting to set. The familiars should be resetting the wards by now. We'd best get moving if we want to catch them in the act."

She nodded, still scowling as she rearranged what clothes had come off while we'd been waiting and moved to join me as I opened the door. I looked around at the massive shelves full of old, dusty tomes and books, half-tempted to stay for just a little while longer to look over them and try and find something of interest.

No time, though.

"Come, we need to get closer," Aliana said softly, taking hold of my arm. I knew what was coming and turned around to try and talk her out of it, but as my mouth opened, the world twisted violently. The corresponding twist as I appeared elsewhere sent me staggering a few steps forward as I realized that we were on one of the tall balconies overlooking Cyron's mansion. I couldn't be sure, but if I had to guess, I would have put a good amount of coin on this being one of the old lookouts used by the Lancers.

"Why can't we ever discuss transporting like that?" I asked, exasperated. "Now we're right over the proverbial lion's jaws, just waiting to get caught, and I have to deal with that as well as the headaches that always come..." I paused for a second, as that last part didn't seem to add up.

Aliana noticed it too and smirked coyly. "There is the possibility of it having something to do with sex. More blood in your little head means less in your bigger one. More tests are required of course, but I'm confident that I'll be pleased with the results."

"Huh," I grunted, raising my eyebrows. I didn't have enough magical knowledge or comprehension of the human body to know if she was right or not, but from what I did know, it did make enough sense to warrant further study. "Wait, what do you mean by more tests?"

She didn't respond, not verbally anyways, tilting her head as her eyes moved down to my cock and back up to my eyes, grinning playfully.

"Oh," I exclaimed, trying to keep my voice lower. "I suppose I should have known that. But yes, I agree, more tests are required."

She grinned and turned back to look down on the mansion. I realized from the location of the central city square in front that it actually was Cyron's. It was different seeing it from above, which was what originally threw me off, but after a few more looks, I realized that we were a lot closer here than we would have been in the library.

"They're resetting the wards, just as you said," Aliana said. I turned, realizing that her eyes were closed. I could see the runes starting to glow softly on her skin, even on her wings.

"I'm still not sure why he does it at sunset," I admitted, dropping into a crouch next to her. "Are there any benefits to doing it at sunset?"

Aliana shrugged. "None that I know of. There is a great deal that isn't known about magic, even by me, however, and assuming that someone as powerful as Cyron does something without any reason for it is a dangerous line of thought to follow and could get us killed."

"Of course," I conceded. "But what are the chances he's just a crackpot, with that and his many other oddities?"

"Considerably higher than the chances of him actually knowing something about magic that I don't," Aliana said. "Back to the topic at hand. I managed to insert us past the wards that are being placed."

"What?" I asked. "How?"

"The young familiar that was placing them had his mind on the young female familiar he was working with," Aliana replied with a gleaming smirk. "All I had to do was distract him with that and push the words into his mouth."

"I hate to sound repetitive here but, again, how?"

I asked. It wasn't shocking, but it certainly sounded like a good trick to learn for later.

"Are you doubting my powers of persuasion?" she asked, licking her lips.

I found that my mouth was suddenly dry and my heart was racing in my chest as I quickly shook my head.

"Good," she said. "Because I've searched around the property and there was only one other part that has wards around it. They're much stronger than those placed around the building, although they are being replaced now, too. In that little room, over there."

She pointed my eyes toward a small tower rising above the rest of the mansion, at the top of which was a small room with one single barred window looking into it. Even from here, the place looked impossible to break into, and I could only imagine that getting closer would reveal it to be more so. To anyone who didn't have a djinn with portal-creating powers on their side, anyways.

"Should we go there now?" I asked.

"Probably not," she replied. "Our familiar is actually trying to engage his would-be paramour in some poor attempts at courtship. It's not going well, but since it seems that they are friends as well, she is trying to let him down gently."

"How can you see all this?" I asked, annoyed at being the single least useful partner in history.

"If you had applied yourself better to your studies, you wouldn't need me to tell you," Aliana replied. "We had plenty of time to learn, after all."

"Less than a month," I snapped back. "How long did it take you to do whatever it is you're doing now?"

Aliana paused, and I could see her runes faltering for a second as she realized I had a good point. I realized in turn that she would never admit it. I grinned as she shook her head.

"That's not the point," she muttered, never glancing away from the room we were looking down on from the balcony, trying not to show the blush that was darkening her cheeks. "The point is, if you applied yourself more, you'd be more than capable of doing this for yourself."

"So, you have faith that I'd have been able to master these techniques faster than you did?" I asked. Sure, it was poking a sleeping bear, but it was still fun to tease her.

"I never said that," Aliana replied, looking up at me. "It's just... if you... Just shut up."

I grinned triumphantly in response as she took a deep breath, trying to focus her mind as she created the portal.

"They're finished arguing," she said softly. "The boy left in a huff, with his lady friend rushing behind, trying to salve his wounded pride. I actually feel a little bad about interfering with their friendship like that."

I shrugged. "It was bound to happen eventually. This way, it didn't fester and get worse to the point where he would have gotten obsessive and vengeful about her not feeling similarly toward him."

"I suppose," Aliana said. "Let's go before they realize that the wards were left unfinished."

I nodded. Even without the headaches, the sensation of twisting through these portals of hers just wasn't pleasant. It was like being washed in a river, beaten on a stone, and wrung dry. Even so, I was looking forward to further testing that might just help me get through this easier. I was putting my puritanical thoughts aside for the moment.

Aliana gripped my wrist and we were dragged through the portal. It still knocked the breath out of me, but as I was getting used to it, I complained less about it on the other side.

My eyes took their time getting adjusted to the darkness around us. I assumed that Cyron was the only one allowed up here, which meant he would be the only one bringing light up here in the first place. I rolled my neck and shoulders as Aliana moved up the steps to the room we'd been watching from the Lancers' tower. There was an old door barring our entry, and I assumed that it was where the wards were placed.

"Any ward worth its salt wouldn't need to be broken each time someone wished to pass it," Aliana explained. "Technically, the person who wove the thing himself would be able to enter and leave without trouble. Interestingly enough, Cyron appears to be the only one allowed into this room. I don't know about you, but I think that sounds rather promising."

"Promising, yes," I said. "How do you propose we get past that same ward, though?"

"Well, as our bickering friends allowed in their distraction, I managed to add a few weaves of my own as they fortified the ward," she replied, stepping up to the door. Wards weren't usually strong enough to be visible, but I could see the effervescent shimmer just in front of the old oak. There weren't many spellcasters capable of something that strong. Not anymore, anyways.

"I couldn't tell you why," she whispered, almost like she was in a trance. "But the weaves of this spell just look so familiar…"

I could see since Aliana's horns dimly illuminated the stairwell we were in, so I couldn't really tell if the shimmer of the ward just peeled away from her hand or if it disappeared altogether. In the end, as she pushed at the door, it opened with a long, loud groan.

We both froze in place, listening with our hearts in our mouths, hoping nobody had heard. When there were no alarms raised in response, we both quickly slipped into the room.

"Should I close the door again?" I asked, tilting my head.

"What would be the point?" she replied. "Besides, we don't want to make that racket again, and I don't want to use any spells that might set the ward off accidentally."

I nodded, agreeing on that bit at least. There had to be all sorts of traps and the like built into this place to make it difficult to get into, but the most difficult part would be navigating the place with just her horns' light for guidance. She wasn't complaining, however, and I didn't want to be the only one, so I followed closely behind her to make sure that if anything was tripped, she would be the one to do it. As far as I could tell, the room was filled with a wide assortment of magical artifacts and trinkets. I wasn't sure what any of them were, but in this light they might as well just be a jumble of useless, if pretty, pieces of jewelry.

"What's this?" she asked, moving over to a book that was on a pedestal, open to one of the chapters and containing writing I couldn't understand.

"I recognize this sigil," she said softly, running her hands over the book, eyes closing and the runes on her arms illuminating as she moved them over the book.

"It's the only other item in here that has been warded on its own," she continued. "It's the same ward that's around the room, so we should be safe."

"Should be?" I asked, tilting my head.

She didn't respond. Her hands were on the book, quickly flipping the pages.

"What does it say?" I asked.

"It's a story," she replied. "But not one that usually reaches the likes of history books. This story should never have been told."

"What is it about?" I asked, my voice softer as I realized that whatever it was had an impact on her, greater than I could understand.

"It's about me," she replied in a monotone. "Well, not only about me, but I do play a part in it. The mighty elf prince Abarat was watching the destruction of our people and knew that something had to be done. He joined forces with the Sisters Three to perform a forbidden rite that was supposed to bring back an army that would protect our people from ultimate destruction, but during the summoning spell we realized he'd tied our fates to the spell but not his. The rite was partially successful, but we were too deeply bound into the magic. It cursed us."

"He used you and your sisters as familiars to protect him should the spell go wrong," I said with a nod. "Which it did, otherwise there would have been no curse. Wait, wait..." I paused, raising my hands to bring the whole line of thought to a halt. "Our people?"

She turned away from the book to look at me. For the first time since I'd met her, I could read alarm in her features, like she'd just given away a secret she'd never meant me to know. I understood. Elves were the reason why there was stigma against magic in the first place, and while they had gone extinct many, many years ago, the thought of them as villains hidden in the woods was still what propelled small children to do their chores and go to bed at the appointed hour.

"You and your sisters are elves?" I asked. I liked to think I was open-minded about such things. Old stories were of little consequence to me. Besides, the stories told about djinn were a lot worse, all things considered, so in practical terms an elf was a massive step up.

"Yes," she replied, looking down. The light in her horns dimmed and her wings drooped. "A very long time ago."

I shook my head, stepping closer and wrapping my arms around her, hugging her close. She seemed surprised by the gesture at first, but quickly squeezed me tighter.

"I know that elves aren't exactly looked at in the

best light these days," I said softly. "But I like to think I know you well enough that any old prejudices can be pushed aside. You've saved my life more times than I can count, and if that's not enough to help me be able to see past some old fairy tales, well, I don't think you would have liked me enough to stick around this long."

She smiled, pulling away and brushing a tear from her eyes. The light in her horns was back, which I took to be a good sign. Her face quickly dropped again, however.

"You don't understand," she said, her voice shaking slightly. "What Abarat, my sisters, and I did that night is the reason why there is so much hatred for my people. It made all the fears humans had of elves come true in the most destructive, horrifying way, and I can't even say they were wrong to think that in the first place."

"We humans aren't such fantastic models of tolerance and wisdom while using magic, either," I said with a shrug. "What you did was a reaction to the actions of my people. You were trying to protect the people you loved. If that's not a good reason to make a bad decision, I really don't know what is."

She smiled but shook her head, trying to push away my attempts at lifting her mood. "Well, I hope you still feel that way, because from what this book is telling me, Cyron is trying to bring Abarat back for one last try at raising that army of his. But this time, Cyron wants it raised for his purposes." For a moment I thought she was going to be sick just from saying that elf's name.

I opened my mouth to say something positive about this turn of events, but nothing was forthcoming.

"Do you think this knowledge will be enough to get your sister to join our side on this?" I asked, tilting my head.

"If not that, then nothing will," Aliana said firmly.

"Perfect," I replied. "Grab that book and let's get out of here."

She looked over at me and then back at the book, hesitating for a moment before taking a breath and lifting the book from the pedestal.

❧ 14 ❧

"**W**hat was that?" I asked, cocking my head and listening.

"Nothing," Aliana replied, looking around the room. "For some reason I thought there might be some kind of binding spell keeping the book in this room. If we take it out, it will try to stop us, or at least warn Cyron that we're here and know what he's doing."

"At this point, he probably already knows about it," I said, keeping my voice low, and listening for anyone who might be coming up the stairs to give us trouble," Either way, I'd say our work here is done. We should take the book and get the fuck out. We can only hope we're not too late to stop whatever it is Cyron is planning. Otherwise, well, we just came all this way for nothing."

Aliana nodded, and I could see her forming the portal. I looked toward the door one more time, honestly looking forward to the jump through the portal more than sticking around this place any longer. Whether it was the dim light or the horde of artifacts didn't really matter. The whole of the place just ticked me off in a way I couldn't comprehend.

We twisted through the portal again, with the gut-wrenching transportation affecting me less than it would have otherwise. I wondered if the pain and discomfort I felt while moving through them was more of a mental thing, but there wasn't time to talk about that now. We had more important matters to discuss.

We came out in the same tower we'd been using to study the mansion. It looked different now that night had fallen. With all the lights, it looked some-what less ominous than it did during the day. I looked down at the ground, trying to get a feel for how far away it was, but was drawn away from that when I saw Aliana dropping into a seat on the floor, her wings fluttering agitatedly.

"What's the matter?" I asked, moving over to sit next to her, bringing my knees up to my chest.

"Reading that book, seeing... remembering what I did back then..." She shook her head, trying to find a way to say it, and clearly struggling. "Memories I thought were buried deep have risen to the surface."

I tilted my head to look her in the eye. "Isn't that usually a good thing?" I asked.

"There was a reason why I put those memories behind me," she explained, sounding almost annoyed with my lack of understanding. "I was a different person then. People I loved died in the fighting and I was feeling hateful and vengeful, to the point of being almost a completely different person. And there was someone else there. Someone... A human. I... why were we in league with a human?"

I leaned closer. I wasn't sure if this was a good idea, but I had to try. I didn't want her to keep floundering like this so I placed my hands on her temples, taking a deep breath as I reached inside myself to find that annoyingly rebellious part of me and push it to the surface, focusing it in my fingers like she'd taught me and closing my eyes.

It was a tentative gesture, one she had to help with as I entered her mind. There was a recurring anger and pain that I could feel in my gut, but as I looked into the picture of the moment she was remembering, there was something odd. True, seeing the world through someone else's mind had to be difficult, but... the world was darker. There was a fire burning, although I couldn't see it. She was looking around in her mind's eye. There were two other women with her. One was Norel, the woman we'd seen in the globe but very different, and the other I didn't recognize. Long, pale hair and pointed ears identified the two as elves. Odd, that wasn't how elves were pictured in history at all.

There was a man in the corner. He looked a good deal more like the villains in the fairy tales we'd been told as children. Large, black eyes, pale skin, long black hair and pointed ears extending out past his head. The runes on his skin were glowing a deep blue, a color I'd never seen in runes before. Maybe it was an elf thing? No, the other two didn't have that. Theirs was a more traditional red. Even so, the power being gathered was almost palpable. I could see it, making the air shudder like reality itself was trying to come to terms with it.

I looked to the corner of the room, and there was, in fact, a man. A human man, with curly brown hair and an elegantly crafted beard. As I looked into his eyes, he moved, turning to see me, tilting his head curiously, like he wasn't just looking at Aliana through her memories.

He could see me and knew it was me he was looking at—and knew who I was, on top of that. He raised his hand, his lips moving. I saw his power starting to arc toward me.

I dropped back, falling away from Aliana with a gasp as I tried to dodge the power of the man reaching for me. I shuddered, trying to get the feeling away as I looked around, just to make sure I was back.

"Are you all right?" Aliana asked. She had horns and wings again. Interesting how it took me a few moments to see her in that form again, like my vision of what she looked like had changed while I was in her head. Well, it would have. She had been an elf once and would have looked differently.

I nodded, scratching my jaw. The fucking beard still itched.

"Call me crazy," I said softly. "But I know who that man was. The human man, not the elf."

She narrowed her eyes. "That's impossible. He wasn't a young man even then. There's no way a human would have survived this long."

"Well, I can't imagine that it's just a coincidence he's the spitting image of Lord Cyron." I replied. "Is that within the realm of possibility?"

Aliana opened her mouth but shut it again, shaking her head. "It's technically possible for a human to extend his or her life through the use of magical rituals and certain artifacts, but it would take someone with immense power and strength to even think of it."

"Someone who might want to help you, your sisters, and that other elf in whatever spell it was you were trying to perform?" I asked, purposely avoiding the use of a name that hadn't sat well with her before.

She nodded. "It makes sense that if he were there, he would have known the story of what happened," she whispered, her voice sounding haunted. "He could have extended his life far beyond his years, but why? Why now, why here? Why was he looking for me?"

"I would imagine he wants the same spell performed," I said, shaking my head. "And he wants as many of the people who performed the original to be part of the encore."

"Norel is in the Emperor's court," Aliana said softly. "She would know him if she saw him. Is she in it with him? No, I can't imagine that. I... She wouldn't. She was cursed, same as I was. Maybe differently, with different results, but still. She has just as much cause to hate him as I do."

"Is he powerful enough to be able to trick her that way?" I asked. "Like that perception field you used."

She tilted her head, thinking. "Well... Maybe. Yes. I suppose that makes sense."

"Shouldn't that be your first thought instead of thinking that your sister, whom I'm guessing you would trust with your life, is in league with one of the people responsible for your current state?" I asked.

She scowled at me, looking more irritated by the fact that I was right than anything else. I smiled and rubbed her shoulders gently in response.

"I can't face her right now," she whispered. "My

mind clearly isn't in the right place for it. If we find her now, I'll just end up shouting at her for something, and then we'll be right back where we started."

I nodded. "Can you think of anywhere we could go where... You're already creating a portal, aren't you?"

She gave me no response, simply taking my hand once it was finished and lurching us through it without any kind of warning or fanfare. I grunted as we dropped back into the very familiar location of the cave we had called home for the past few weeks.

"I had a couple of ideas, actually," I complained, rubbing some feeling back into my ass. "Somewhere that might have an actual bed we hadn't done away with before leaving this place to cover our tracks. And maybe a razor."

"Did any of those places take kindly to housing a djinn with wings and horns?" Aliana asked, sitting cross-legged on the ground in front of me, looking up with a cheeky smile.

"That's a good point," I admitted. "I want to be rash and I know you do as well. It's probably a better idea not to crash through the city with blood and vengeance on our minds before we know what we're trying to avenge in the first place."

She chuckled, looking at me for a moment before leaning her head on my shoulder. I slipped my hand around her waist and pulled her closer. She placed a light kiss on my cheek before we lay down on the spot that had been our bed before. It was still reasonably soft and would do in a pinch since we needed sleep. She lay facing me this time, pressing her face into my chest, and was soon fast asleep. It took me a little while longer.

Sure, memories of the night in her bath and just earlier that same afternoon made sure that my mind was on the arousal I was trying to conceal, but there was something different now, too. The way she pressed herself into me pulled a warm feeling from the pit of my gut, one that wasn't completely about sex, I realized. I wanted her that way too, but there was something different now. The world hadn't been a kind place for her. Annoyingly enough, considering she was more capable of taking care of herself than I was, it didn't change the fact that I wanted to keep her away from everything that was causing her pain by protecting her, holding her and making it all right again.

I threaded my fingers through her hair, smiling. Here I was, fighting for my life and discovering a plot of unknown magnitude that was about to change the world forever. Was now really the time to fall in love?

❦ 15 ❦

My eyes shot open at the sound of a piercing scream. I tried to move around, looking for any sign of danger around us, but there was none. No sudden movements, no glint of steel in the dim light of the moon coming from outside the cave. The scream was a lot softer than I thought it had been, too. I looked down, seeing that Aliana was gripping my shirt tight enough that my neck was starting to be pulled down. I could feel hot tears soaking into it, too. I pulled her closer and ran my fingers through her hair.

"Aliana," I whispered, gently nudging her to wake up. She gasped, speaking in a language I didn't understand as I shook her again, trying to get a response out of her. She shook her head, opening her eyes and jerking away from me for a moment, like she hadn't expected to see me.

"What's the matter?" I asked, pulling her back in and wrapping my arms around her shoulders, avoiding the touch of her wings for the moment as I leaned in closer. "Were you having a nightmare?"

She was awake now, but there were still tears coming from her eyes. I could feel her nails digging into my ribs as she gripped me tighter, her body racked with sobs as she buried her head in my chest. I didn't want to pry, but there was a low, dirty feeling in my chest. She was in pain, and when someone I cared for was in pain, it was my job to make them feel better again. As it stood, I felt rather helpless. I wanted to help, but I didn't know how. It wasn't a new feeling for me, but that didn't really take the sting out of it.

"I'm sorry," she whispered, her voice hoarse. "I... The dream, I can't shake it."

"Don't apologize," I said softly, stroking her hair tenderly and holding her close. Maybe this—be someone she could rely on to help her get through moments like these—was all I could do to help. I couldn't imagine she'd had too many people like that over the years. Being alone was a terrifying prospect, and my own experience wasn't nearly as profound as hers in that respect.

"My sisters were there," she whispered, her voice vibrating into my chest as she did. "We were together at last. Everything was the way it was before. All was forgiven and in the past. We were all just enjoying each other's company and then something happened. I can't remember what, but we were separated again, and I couldn't stand it happening. If something were to happen to Norel before we could reach her, I would never forgive myself for that."

I nodded. I knew where this was going, and I didn't want to sound anything less than supportive.

"Do you have a plan?" I asked, still stroking her hair.

She pulled away to look me in the eye. "You mean beyond teleporting over to where I can find her through the globe?"

I nodded. "How would you plan on breaking the news to her that Cyron is trying to bring an evil elf prince back to life and restart an ancient spell that you said was only marginally successful to begin with?"

She sighed, shaking her head. "I have no idea. I don't even know what I'm going to say to her when I see her, only... I have to do it now."

I looked at Aliana. I knew I was no pleasant sight to look at, wearing ragged servant's clothes. Aliana, while gorgeous, didn't seemed to be dressed the way any lady of standing, which Norel was apparently trying to be, would see as appropriate. Of course, if Aliana really meant now, we would have to rely on the woman recognizing her and overlooking me entirely.

I sighed, pushing myself out of our 'bed' and groaning as the effects of sleeping on what was really just the cold hard floor of a cave left my muscles tense and unresponsive. I stretched, trying to get them moving again as Aliana jumped lightly to her feet. Despite the nightmares, she looked perfectly rested, certainly more so than I felt, and more than ready to jump into action.

"So, your plan?" I asked, noting that the sky outside was already starting to turn a delicate shade of pink, announcing that sunrise would be with us shortly. The cover of night would not be with us for too much longer.

"I know where she is," Aliana said softly. "She would be asleep in her manse, or feigning it, anyway. We could slip in during the change of the guard, and find our way to where she is from there."

"Wait," I said, shaking my head. "We can use a portal to enter the house of a man who is clearly a lot more powerful than anyone else in the empire. Why can't we portal into her room to find her without having to deal with a changing of the guard, or anything like it?"

"Cyron is powerful, yes, but his technique is

limited as well as his knowledge of the various powers that I have at my disposal," Aliana replied, shaking her head. "Norel will have no such encumberments. Her manse will be considerably more difficult to infiltrate."

I nodded. "Right. Well, then, changing of the guard, what next?"

"One step at a time, Grant," Aliana said with a smile, taking my hand.

"Damn." I started, feeling the air rushing from my lungs as we twisted through space for a second that seemed to last forever.

"... it!" I completed when we dropped back into reality, shaking my head. I was starting to miss the headaches. It seemed like they were all that was keeping Aliana from transporting us anywhere in the damn world that she pleased. There were no such restrictions now, and it took me a moment to quell the nausea that was rising up in my stomach.

"Quit your whining," Aliana said softly. "We're here."

"How long until the changing of the guard?" I asked, looking around. We were somewhere near the center of town since I could hear the clamoring of the bells, alerting the men guarding the walls that it was time to open the gates, but the precise location was harder to tell.

No, not that much harder, I realized. The stench

of open sewers, cattle, and pigs was enough to tell me we were in the Slums. What we were doing here was more of a mystery.

"Long enough for us to change," Aliana said with a grin.

"Into wha—gods damn it." She disappeared into another portal before I could finish my question, and I was left in what looked like the courtyard of a villa long abandoned by its previous owners. *That was odd,* I thought. I never knew the Slums had any villas.

I paced around for a few more seconds as I watched the sky turn from pink to red, with streaks of orange painting across it. Sunrise was upon us, and the changing of the guard was less than half an hour away. I ground my teeth, looking around.

I heard a snap and crackle of the air parting as a twitch of movement caught my eye. I turned around to see Aliana returning, a pair of packs in her hands. I tilted my head questioningly as she dropped them on the ground, the sound of plate armor ringing making my eyebrows raise.

"Armor?" I asked.

"Not just any armor," she said with a grin, peeling the leather back to reveal steel painted in black and red. "Lancers' armor."

"Well, color me impressed," I said, not a trace of sarcasm in my voice. The Lancers' armor was made by the finest blacksmiths in the empire, with protection runes to keep from breaking and to make sure that arrows and crossbow bolts did not pierce. As such, they were very closely guarded by the men who wore it, since they would not suffer the touch of any other men on it.

"I do have a question, though," I said, dropping into a crouch. "Assuming that this armor fits us—and with your horns and wings, I can assure you that it will not—what do you plan on us accomplishing, wearing these pieces?"

"I can make them fit," Aliana said with a smile. "For one, the armor I picked out for myself is that of the scouts, which has a leather hood instead of a helmet and a bit more room between the plates for my wings. And for two, this is only to keep us from catching anyone's attention. People do tend to look down and away when they see anyone wearing this armor, not wanting to catch the attention of the men who could send them to what they all assume is going to be their life's greatest torment, so they do anything they can not to be noticed. Odd how people feel more afraid than comforted when met with the sight of the men who are supposed to keep them safe, is it not?"

I nodded. Then again, the Lancers weren't around to keep them safe, but rather to serve the Emperor's interests and keep *him* safe, making it a good deal more difficult to trust them.

We both dressed quickly. The armor was a lot lighter than it looked. A testament to its makers, I assumed. We walked out of the villa, with Aliana putting on a hood and cloak to cover her more distinguishing features. With her field of altered perception in place, almost nobody saw us. Those who did by coming inside the field, quickly looked away and stepped out, trying not to attract attention, as she had predicted.

My armor was a little too large around the shoulders and arms, making my movements awkward and nosier than I would have liked, but even so, nobody gave us a second glance. We were back in the nobler sections of the city before too long, and it was an even shorter walk to reach the area I remembered from looking into her globe. It was a smaller mansion, on the border section of the area where nobles lived. This was where more recent additions to the gentry set up their houses.

Which meant it hadn't been that long since Norel had joined them.

I looked around, keeping my eyes on our surroundings as the rest of the Lancers started to move away from their posts and march off. None of them gave us a second glance either, all bound by oath or whatever it was that kept them on their path.

I kept my eyes pointed forward the same as they were, trying not to draw attention. I wasn't sure if there were any who might be able to see through this field of hers, and the fact that we were walking around in bright daylight was making me a lot more nervous about what we were doing.

We slipped into the building, avoiding the worried glances of the servants. They looked terrified to see us. I looked at Aliana, wondering what it was we were doing here, or what we were looking for.

We veered through the building, which was impossibly larger than it appeared from the outside and formed a maze that I just couldn't understand.

"She loved mazes," Aliana replied, reading where my mind was going as I was looking around. "We never understood how she made them, but they guided people the way she wanted them to go. Or did you think it was a coincidence that you found me in ruins that Cyron and your master needed a piece of magical parchment in order to navigate?"

I looked around. "Did she make those ruins for you?"

"No," Aliana replied as she moved through the halls. "I just knew that she built them, and I needed a place to hide."

I looked around the place, following her through it. "How come she isn't guiding us to her?" I asked.

"Because she doesn't know we're here," she

replied, looking around, tugging me to the left, guiding me through a doorway into a room with a window that was illuminated by the soft touch of candlelight and the sun just starting to peek over the horizon.

There was a woman sitting at a desk. She had green hair, similar to Aliana's, but she was relatively petite. She was dressed in silver and purple, with a silver tiara gracing her brow. This had to be Norel.

She looked up as we entered. She barely paid me a second glance, but her gaze lingered on Aliana. She rose from her seat. She was shorter than Aliana by a solid foot, yet she carried herself with a kind of grace that told me that she was used to looking down on people no matter how tall they were. More or less the way she'd barely looked at me.

"Ali?" Norel asked, the composed face she wore breaking a little. There was a single tear running down her cheek, a twitch of a smile of her lips, like there were a hundred different emotions rushing through her mind and she was having a hard time trying to get a grip on them.

"Norel!" Aliana said, rushing forward, pushing her hood down and reaching out to embrace her sister, but in the split second before contact, Norel took a step backward, her eyes widening like she had latched onto a single emotion, which was terror.

I looked around, gripping my fists, anticipating

the sight of Lancers—real Lancers—to come rushing to carry us away to the tower for a very short lifetime of torture and pain.

"You're dead," Norel said softly. "He said you were dead."

I tilted my head, seeing tears running down Aliana's cheeks. She looked like she was trying to hold herself back from reaching out to hug her sister once more.

"Well, I'm not," Aliana said, her voice cracking. "He lied to you. Was it Cyron? He lied, Nor, please, you have to believe me. Please..."

Norel blinked, all the different emotions still sorting through her head as she stared Aliana down. The terror was still dominant on her face, however.

"He lied to you, Nor. Please," Aliana said, trying to fight back her sobs. "I've been stuck in a ring as a fucking djinn ever since that horrible night. He lied to us then, tried to use us, and he's been lying to you ever since. Please... Nor..."

Another tear joined the first. Norel suddenly looked at me, almost shocked, like she'd forgotten I was there. I couldn't really blame her, all things considered.

She turned back to face Aliana. "Touch, please. I need to know that you don't lie." Her voice was soft, high-pitched, and yet still commanding in presence.

Aliana turned to me, grabbing my hand purposefully and dragging me closer to Norel, who took my other hand. Aliana and Norel each took the other's remaining hand, completing the circle. I looked around at both of them, but I was clearly not the focus of whatever this was supposed to be.

Just a familiar, I thought, *helping all this along.*

Memories of the burning, torturous touch inside my head from Vis' poking around, to Aliana's warm and arousing style, turned my mind to the icy and clinical touch from Norel's thoughts pressing into my mind. The invasion was faster, sharper. I almost didn't feel it until she was already deep inside, pushing around, finding all my thoughts about Aliana and glancing over them. The thoughts of what happened in the tub, and again in the library, were looked into very briefly. The connection went both ways, like all the others, causing a stunned silence in the connection between Aliana and Norel. There wasn't much embarrassment from Aliana. Norel moved past it without comment.

As quickly as she was in, she was out again. I could see a light sheen of sweat coating her skin as she pulled away, quickly arranging her features, wiping the sweat from her face to keep it from ruining her makeup.

"Well," Norel gasped. It wasn't just sweat on her face, I realized. There were tears. They had been streaming freely all throughout what we'd been doing.

"It's really you." Norel turned to Aliana, who was doing all she could not to break down. Norel stepped in before Aliana dropped to the ground, picking her up and holding her close. "I thought I'd lost you forever."

❧ 16 ❧

"**A**s much as I hate to interrupt this reunion," I said, "there is the matter of what Cyron might have planned."

"Oh, right," Aliana said, disentangling herself as the two sisters pulled apart. There were more than a few words that needed to be said between the two of them, and the tears they brought had been pouring for the past few minutes. I really did feel bad about parting them, but we did have a couple of more pressing matters that needed to be attended to first.

"Yes, I remember," Norel said softly, nodding and quickly rearranging her hair. She did that a lot, I realized. Constantly caring for how she looked and how she appeared. I shook my head, bringing my mind back to the matter at hand.

"I take it you saw what we discovered during your

rooting around in our minds?" I asked, looking at Norel.

She nodded and inhaled deeply. "Cyron has some intention of bringing him back to the surface." She turned to Aliana. "Do you think he's planning on trying that same spell again?"

"Well, he's had you around," I said, knowing I was by no means an expert in any of this, but still wanting my input out there. "He was looking for Aliana when I ran into her."

"In more ways than one," Norel said.

"And what's that supposed to—" Aliana asked, looking at her sister, but I stepped in before the loving reunion could turn into fighting.

"Not important at the moment," I said in a soft comforting voice as I placed my hand on Aliana's shoulder, pulling her a step away from Norel. "I was their unwitting pawn in all that, and it ended up proving unprofitable for them to let me into it without actually telling me what was happening..."

"Stay on track, Grant," Aliana chided, nudging me gently in the shoulder.

I nodded in response. "Right. So, considering that he was looking to gather all but one of the members of those who were there for the original spell, it just makes sense that he's going to try it again. What was the purpose of the spell, anyways?"

Aliana looked at Norel, who looked away quickly.

"I don't want to say," Norel said softly. "It was a terrible time, and in the heat of war, you lose sight of what might be important regarding morals and character. You end up doing anything that needs to be done to win, and in the end, that was a defeat in and of itself."

I took a deep breath, trying not to rush her. It was clearly a very emotional and dark moment in both their pasts, but as of right now, I had no judgement to pass. What the hell did I know about the choices that had to be made during wartime?

"It was a spell to open the underworld," Norel said, sensing my impatience, looking over at Aliana. "The reason we attempted it was because there was a legend of a powerful army that could be summoned to fight for the elves in our ever more desperate battle for survival. Oh... You..." She looked over at Aliana. I shrugged.

"I already know that the two... er, three, of you were elves," I said. Something just wasn't right. It was early morning, and I remembered hearing the sounds of birds chirping and singing outside the window. They'd gone silent now. That, or it was no longer early morning and the birds had moved away. I wasn't sure which was more likely, since I had no idea how long we'd been here.

"Well, then," Aliana said, sensing my uncomfortableness as well as its source.

"What do we know about what he's trying to do?" I asked.

"The spell has to happen during a solar eclipse," Norel said, shaking her head. "The coalition of the two heavenly entities increases the amount of power to be reaped from one's surroundings, making for the only time when such a spell would even be possible."

I looked up to the window again, hearing a low... something. It wasn't quite a growl. It sounded like one, or something like it.

"Get away from the window," I said suddenly, tugging Aliana back a few steps. She looked at me, almost annoyed, but then both she and Norel sensed it too. They might even know what it was, but all I could feel was an impending sense of dread as the sound started to grow closer and louder. All three of us quickly backed away from the window, moving toward the door a second before the building collapsed around us as something truly massive crashed through the walls like they were made of hay.

They weren't, and the building soon collapsed around it, giving it pause. We moved away from the building for fear that it would collapse on us, too, but I could still see it moving through the rubble. Whatever it was, it was made some something shiny and black. Well, partly shiny, I realized as it moved out from under the rubble, and partly glowing. It's skin, if that was what I could call it, was covered in magical runes, all much more complicated than anything I'd ever seen. That wasn't really saying much, admittedly, but there was still some powerful magic radiating from this creature.

As it finally managed to untangle itself from the rubble, I could see that it was made in the shape of a massive hound. It even had short, pointed ears and powerful, muscular shoulders with lean hindquarters, giving it the look of a hunting dog. Except that it was the size of a horse and its eyes were glowing red.

"Fuck me in the ass," I hissed, looking around for something like a weapon that I could use, but finding only a piece of wood from Norel's desk. It wasn't much of a weapon, but it was long enough that it could be used as a short polearm, and there was a sharp point on it. I looked back up as the creature started trying to track us down again.

"What the fuck is that?" I asked, looking over at Aliana. She had her dagger in hand and she was spinning it artfully between her fingers in the way she did when she was looking at a fight. Norel had no such weapons, but the lightning arcs I could see jumping from her fingers told me that she was far from unarmed in this fight.

Much better armed than I was, at any rate.

"That is an obsidian canine," Norel said. "Haven't seen one of those in a long time."

"A hellhound," Aliana said, explaining for my benefit. "Summoned from another realm."

"Well, then," I said, gripping my pointed stick tighter as the creature cocked its head, seemingly following the sound of our voices. "How do we kill it?"

"You can't," Norel said, rolling her neck. "There isn't a metal on earth that can pierce its skin."

"Doesn't mean we won't give it the old profession-al's try, though," Aliana said with a grin, her wings flapping lightly with excitement. "We trained for this, Grant. Remember what I taught you. Keep moving, stay aware of your surroundings and don't lose your footing. Find a weak spot and more importantly, have fun." She finished that sentence with a wide grin on her face as she started running to my left. Norel took off to my right, leaving me in the middle with nothing but a sharpened stick and ill-fitting armor.

"Why couldn't she have found some weapons to go with the armor?" I grumbled to myself. The hound seemed to focus on me as an easier target and started advancing, picking up speed as it ran over the rubble of the house that it had almost fully destroyed in its lashing about. What was left of the house was crum-bling as the creature's weight made the ground shake with each step.

"Wow, you are a big motherfucker," I said, waiting until the last moment before jumping to the side, making sure to avoid any of the fallen debris as I fell on my shoulder, struggling to regain my feet as the hound landed where I'd been less than a second earlier. It skidded across the ground as it tried to pull itself to a halt. *That was what came with giving a creature obsidian skin,* I mused. *The traction had to be terrible.*

That said, it twisted around quickly, finding me and charging again.

Suddenly, my ears were ringing as a lightning bolt arced across the sky, striking the hound's head. The force of the strike knocked it onto its back, but as it quickly regained its feet, I realized that the strike that would have killed at least a dozen men had done little in the way of lasting damage, even as sparks continued to fly from the creature's skin.

As it tried to recover, I saw Aliana jumping down from one of the pieces of building that was still standing. While it didn't seem like her wings helped her fly, they did perform the act of gliding rather well, I realized, as she cleared a fifteen-foot leap with the smooth, practiced grace of an acrobat. She sailed through the air to land on the creature's shoulders, leaning down to hammer her blade into the creature's neck.

It had no effect other than letting off a massive spray of sparks from the impact, but left no sign of a dent on the creature's skin. The hound let out a surprisingly feline roar, trying to reach around to bite at Aliana. When that failed, it jumped into the air, trying to dislodge her.

It succeeded, but as it looked around for her, I realized she'd made use of her wings again and was sailing away to what was hopefully a safe distance. Another bolt of lightning struck the hellhound's face, distracting it momentarily to allow Aliana to land safely, but it tracked her down quickly. Another lightning bolt from Norel failed to distract it again as it bounded heavily over to where Aliana was still trying to regain her feet. Massive teeth caught the light as it tried to bite her. Luckily, she threw up a hasty shield to block its attack, which disappeared in another shower of sparks as soon as the creature was pushed aside.

I looked around, feeling utterly useless as I held onto my pathetic piece of wood, looking around for something I could do. There had to be something, after all. Something I could do to help.

Look for a weakness.

I blinked. I could do that. It was distracted right now, with Aliana throwing her shields up in a desperate attempt to keep the biting creature at bay. I gripped my stick tighter, moving closer to it. For some reason, I was only now noticing the heat radiating off it, and that its low growling resembled the sound I'd heard before the building fell around it just minutes before.

A weakness. The only cracks appearing on its skin were the runes I assumed were keeping it alive. That was as close to an opening as I was going to get, I mused, leaning closer, putting all my weight behind the stick as I smashed it into the runes.

They were too fine for the now-slightly-blunted piece of wood I was using, but the sparks flew out harder than with the knife or lightning strikes, which told me that I was onto something.

Unfortunately, I realized that I'd just successfully drawn its attention away from Aliana as the massive, glowing eyes turned to me, obsidian lips peeling back to show a long row of very sharp matching teeth.

It spun around faster than I would have believed, jaws violently snapping at me. I just barely avoided having my torso chomped on as I dropped backward, hitting the ground on my back. I struggled, scooting myself across the ground as quickly as I could as the creature turned fully. *It was very easily distracted*, I thought.

My breath was knocked out of me as teeth sank easily through the armor I was still wearing, biting into my leg.

"Fuck!" I screamed in pain, lashing out as quickly as I could, hammering the pointed piece of wood into the creature's glowing eye. The roar was a lot louder this time, or seemed like it since it was now vibrating into my thighbone as the creature dropped to the ground with its jaw still clamped onto my leg.

I was really good at finding these weak spots, I thought, trying to keep my mind off the mind-numbing agony and the terrifying thought that the smell of seared flesh was actually coming from me. I screamed again, pushing the stake deeper and deeper into the creature's eye. It seemed to be in immense pain but wouldn't let my leg go.

"A little help, please?" I screamed at the other two, who seemed to have stopped in their tracks to watch what was happening. They snapped into action. I could see Norel building up another charge of lightning into her fingers as Aliana jumped forward.

"Hit the fucking runes!" I roared, trying to let the pain fuel the anger that was rushing like fire through my veins as I kept pushing the stick deeper into the creature's eye. The heat coming from it started to make the piece of wood smoke, then catch fire.

Flames started licking at my fingers. Everything in me was begging me to let go but the knowledge that if I did, it would be back up to kill me and my friends in no time kept me pushing the wood deeper as I pinned its head to the ground, gritting my teeth and trying to ignore the agony of the fire. I finally let go with one hand. It dropped and landed on the creature's skin, which was hotter, it seemed, than the flames that were consuming my stake. I snapped my hand away, looking around to see what was taking Aliana and Norel so damn long to do something.

Aliana dropped in, screaming what sounded like a battle cry as she hammered her dagger into the hound's chest. The dagger, much sharper than my piece of wood, dug easily into the runes and pushed deeper, all the way up to the hilt. Aliana jumped away.

"Now!" she called. I had no idea what she wanted me to do now, but then Norel stepped closer, her eyes glowing with the amount of power she'd taken into herself. She pushed her hands forward, releasing her most powerful lightning bolt yet, channeling it through Aliana's dagger and into the hound.

For a moment, all the runes went dead, the fire in its eyes disappearing as the power of the bolt was absorbed into its body. And then it shattered into a thousand tiny obsidian pieces.

I let out a whining cry of pain, looking at my burned hands. The one that had settled on the creature's skin had the runes seared into it. It would have been an interesting study if my mind was capable of thinking about anything other than the amount of pain I was in.

"Grant!" Aliana cried, jumping over the pile of obsidian shards and coming over to me. "Are you all right?"

"Peachy," I gasped through gritted teeth, looking down at my leg. The ruined armor covered most of the damage, but from the amount of blood that was spilling through the tooth marks in the steel plates, it couldn't be good.

"Lie down," Norel said, her cool voice coming as more of a comfort than the terrified look on Aliana's face, oddly enough. I did as she said as she quickly started tugging the pieces of ruined armor away from my leg. I had thought the pain couldn't get any worse. I was wrong. I gritted my teeth again, masking the scream that came up from my gut with a growl as I writhed in agony.

"Lie still," Norel commanded smoothly.

"I have an idea." That pain-stealing anger rose in me again. "Why don't you get wounded and I'll start treating your wounds and telling you to lie fucking still?"

"That doesn't make any sense," Norel pointed out calmly.

"I know!" I hissed, trying to do as she told me. I couldn't stand to look at the damage, wondering if dying would be a relief from this. I'd read about people being in so much pain that they wanted to die —I had to be getting close to that threshold without quite reaching it. I wanted the pain to go away, but not enough to die and leave Aliana behind to deal with all this without me.

I was stubborn like that.

It took me a moment to realize the pain in my leg was starting to recede, pulling away, almost like it was being sucked out of the wounds. I pulled myself up, watching the damage on my leg start to disappear where Norel had her hands on it. There were arcs of white energy in her fingers that were pressing into me. I took a deep breath, trying to close my eyes, but at the same time very curious about the nature of the magic she was using.

I realized I was holding my breath and inhaled deeply, trying to understand what was happening. My mind was going wobbly, for lack of a better word, at the relief from the pain.

"He's going into shock," Norel said to Aliana.

"No, I'm not," I gasped, blinking and trying to stay awake.

Huh, maybe I was. It certainly beat the hell out of having to wallow in misery.

I was brought back to the moment as Aliana leaned in, pressing her lips to mine. My eyes took a moment to focus, all my senses coming to full alert as I reached up to stroke her hair, my burned hands dropping as I shrieked in pain.

"Well, that works, I suppose," Norel said with an icy tone. "His leg should be fine, if a little tender."

"What about my hands?" I asked, displaying the angry red welts on them to her.

"Huh," she grunted, leaning in closer to the hand that had runes seared into it. "That's odd. I haven't seen runes like that in years. We should probably study them when we have the time."

"That's not what I meant." I looked down at the leg she'd just taken the time to heal. The wound was gone, though it was interesting to see just how the hound's teeth had warped the metal armor she'd removed, like the heat coming from the beast's mouth had been hot enough to melt steel.

That was a terrifying thought.

The wounds were gone, but the hair on my legs had been singed off. The whole of that part of my leg looked fresh and pink, and, as she had said, tender. I winced, moving the muscles. There was a phantom pain, like my leg was remembering what it felt like when a horse-sized hound had been gnawing on it, but I assumed it would pass soon.

I pushed myself to my feet, wincing as my hands throbbed in pain.

"Well, then," Norel said with a smile. "I can't say I'm impressed with your magical abilities, but I must commend you on your courage."

"About that." Aliana frowned. "Why didn't you reach for your powers? I thought that was what we spent all that time practicing for."

"We spent less than a month getting me to use powers that are as elusive to me as they are to those who wanted to use them," I said. "The rest of my life was spent learning to live without those same powers. When the time came to put my life on the line, well, I still need more practice, and we have better things to worry about."

"Right," Norel said. "As if we needed any kind of indication, the hellhound's presence is enough to tell us that Cyron is already advancing his plans."

"Didn't you say he needed an eclipse for that?" I asked.

"Well, yes," Norel said, taking my hands in hers, the same healing energy starting to flow into the welts on them and my arms. "But he should know the two of you broke in by now, since you took his book. He's just stupid enough and in enough of a hurry to try it anyway."

"Let him," Aliana said with a snort. "Let the magic tear him apart."

"Don't be stupid, Ali," Norel snapped. "Even if he fails, which wouldn't be a given considering the amount of power he's accumulated over the years, the failure of the spell could still send this whole city and much, much more into a fiery pit. While I am one to approve of the hunt for vengeance, I think that might be taking it a bit far, don't you?"

"You haven't changed at all," Aliana noted, rolling her eyes, which told me that she knew her sister was right but didn't quite like being talked down to like that.

In all honesty, I wasn't too fond of it either, but that would have to be handled another time.

"I have to go to him," Norel said, pulling away from my hands, leaving them similarly healed, if similarly tender to the touch. "Cyron, I mean. He still thinks I'm on his side and has no reason to think otherwise. I can get close enough to stop him."

"Now who's being stupid?" I asked, looking down at my hands. "How come you left the welts with the runes on them?"

"Like I said, I wish to study them," Norel said, taking a step toward me. "And I beg your pardon?"

"That hound came to your house," I said, still staring at the runes. "It attacked *your* house, which you were in. I mean, even if he just sent it to track Aliana and me down, he has to know where it was and make the connection. He might be stupid enough to try some world-ending spell, but I have to think he's smart enough to realize that."

It was amusing how Aliana and Norel both had the same look when they knew someone was right but still didn't approve of their tone. I tried not to let my amusement reach my face, however.

"I suppose you're right," Norel said, grudgingly. "I still think we need to find Cyron, to stop him."

"Where would he be?" Aliana asked.

"He wouldn't want to conduct any spells in his home," Norel said, looking around. "We have to go. We may be too late already."

I didn't want to point out that if we were already too late, it wouldn't really matter if we hurried or not. It was better to keep our minds on the positive side, after all.

We picked our way through the rubble, climbing over the remains of Norel's house. There was still a lot of it on its feet, but there was going to be a lot of work put into making it livable once more. I'd thought that the sight of a massive hound tearing a mansion down would have attracted a bit of a crowd, but as we reached the edge of Norel's property and got out to the street again, the place was deserted. Well, that made sense too, I supposed. Nobody would want to stick around in case the massive hound decided to attack them instead. Without a word, we started heading toward Cyron's mansion.

"On the off chance that Cyron has already started the spell, and considering the death toll expected whether he succeeds or fails," Aliana said, as we moved through a suddenly and uncharacteristically abandoned marketplace. "Do you suppose we should start evacuating the city? Save as many lives as we can?"

I opened my mouth to reply when the earth started shaking. Just a gentle tremor at first, but it quickly built in intensity until it was all the three of us could do just to remain on our feet. There was an explosion, far enough away that we weren't close enough to be caught in the blast, and yet close enough that it knocked the three of us to the ground. It knocked most of the rickety market stands down too, as well as a handful of walls and buildings.

I was the first to my feet, looking around to make sure everyone was all right. Aliana was up next, scowling and saying something in elfish that had to be a curse as she grabbed my hand. I didn't even complain this time as we were pulled and twisted into the portal that spat us out on the lookout tower above the Lancers' guardhouse we'd been on the day before. The city looked different now. I could see the smoke rising from fires all across it, and the sounds of screaming were easily heard from all points in the expansive city below us. The tromping of booted feet could also be heard below as the Lancers were quickly organizing, though what they were organizing for wasn't quite clear.

"You're right," I said. "We need to help them."

Aliana nodded, but I didn't think she'd heard me. All her attention seemed to be focused on the source of the explosion. There were more than a few houses and mansions leveled in the blast, but there was one at the epicenter. The mansion itself was large enough that it wasn't all knocked down, but a whole wing of it was just gone in favor of a massive crater.

There was something moving inside that crater—crawling out of it, in fact. It was massive, even from our removed standpoint. Vaguely humanoid, with arms, legs, and a head, but it was a brown color, with pieces of it dropping away with each movement. It was large enough to be able to maintain its form even so.

"That's a—" Aliana started, and I nodded.

"I know what that is," I cut her off. Unlike elves and djinn, golems were very much the stuff of reality, even if they should have been confined to nightmares. Mostly banned from use across the empire, they were creatures of rock and clay, following the commands of their summoner without question. Destruction and chaos followed in their wake, with the death toll of their use in battle being astonishing enough to make the Emperor himself, usually quite fond of large, dull creatures that followed orders without question, ban them personally.

I turned around, wondering if we were going to start helping the people closest to the creature to escape, when I saw a tiny little man standing near it. Even from here, I could see the distortions of reality and the glowing runes that came from the power needed to control the beast. I could see his mouth moving but couldn't make out the words.

"Cyron," I said. "That's got to be him."

"Agreed." Aliana's voice devoid of emotion. I turned to look at her, but she was only in my vision for a moment before disappearing into a portal.

"Gods... damn it." I shook my head. "And just how the fuck does she think I'm going to get down from here?"

❧ 17 ❧

I found a way down from the tower, mostly because it seemed like the Lancers had more to worry about outside than someone who had managed to break into their precious building. Besides, I was still wearing what Lancer armor hadn't been damaged by the massive hound so I wasn't worth a single glance from the men rushing about, much less two.

I reached the courtyard and beyond in a few minutes. A good deal had changed while I'd been navigating the Lancers' guardhouse. Back in the old days, I had always feared getting captured and locked up there, so I had the exits of the building committed to memory, just in case.

The old days were less than a month ago, I realized. How was that possible? It felt like decades.

I looked around, expecting the monster to be

tearing his way through the city, proving the prohibitions of their use very well-founded. But my quick look over the city revealed no new leveled buildings, and while there was still pandemonium and chaos all around, there wasn't a massive golem adding to it anywhere in sight.

That was, until I heard, or rather felt, the massive footfalls thudding on the ground. The problem of having something that large in your thrall was how easy it was to track it. I circled around, trying to see where it was going, and wasn't sure why I was surprised when I saw it heading deeper and deeper into the forest. The same forest I'd run into when I stole the scroll from Pollock. The same one I'd found Aliana in.

I didn't believe in coincidences.

Norel came running up to me, looking around. "Grantham. You're Grantham, right?"

"Yes, yes, but Grant is better," I replied, looking at her. "Didn't you recognize me?"

"Oh please, Grant." She smiled as she added, "All you humans look alike. I mistook a couple of the damned Lancers for you. Talk about an interesting conversation. But never mind that, where is my sister?"

I looked out into the forest, where the golem was marching, pulling down trees in his wake.

"Where do you think?" I asked.

"No need to be snide," she said. "Why didn't you stop her? You know she can't take one of those down on her own."

"What in our admittedly short history together makes you think I could stop her?" I asked as we started running into the forest, following the wide path left by the creature.

"A valid point," Norel conceded.

We made our way deeper inside, seeing the kind of destruction a golem could cause when destruction wasn't even on its mind as we started sprinting toward where it had stopped. The ground was still shaking. As we got closer, it looked like the massive thing was digging into the earth. I had no idea where we were, but I could make an educated guess as to why it had picked that spot. It had to be somewhere near those old ruins.

A creature that large had to be hard to miss but as we started getting closer to where the thudding was coming from, there was no sign of it. Not at first anyways. As we got closer, a massive hole in the ground indicated where it had gone.

"Well then," I said, trying to catch my breath. "I don't suppose we should wait here and gather our forces, maybe look for Aliana before going down into the tunnels to fight a golem and, I assume, Cyron?"

"She's already down there," Norel said, shaking her head. "We have to help her."

"Of course, she is," I said, still trying to recover my breath. "I don't suppose you know how to open a portal that can take us down there without having to fall?"

Norel sighed, nodding and taking my hand in hers. The twisting and pulling from her portal was oddly gentler than Aliana's. Either way, we ended up at the bottom of the hole all the same. There was light from a handful of lit torches, I realized, illuminating what had to be a massive room. Aliana was there, dagger drawn, flitting around the room, using her legs and wings to good effect as she fought with Cyron, who had a sword in his hands. It was gleaming with runes, meant for the blade's protection, I assumed. The runes were glowing hotly, showering the room with sparks each time the sword connected with something.

"You need to help her," Norel said. "I'll take the golem."

"A better idea," I said, stopping her. "Since the golem is busy doing something else," it was digging for something in the middle of the room, "you head back to the city and make sure that everybody is removed from where they might be killed if things go poorly here."

"The chances of things going poorly increase if I go," Norel said with a warning tone in her voice. "Help Aliana. I'll try to slow the golem down."

I nodded. There wasn't much chance of me stopping her from doing what she wanted, anyway. Besides, it wasn't like she was wrong. I just felt bad about leaving that many people in the wake of the destruction that would happen if we failed.

Norel was already on the move, heading toward the corner of the room where the golem was as I moved over to where Aliana was attacking Cyron. She seemed to have the upper hand, though, and I wasn't sure what exactly I was going to be able to do to help. I had no stick, my powers were still as hard to use as they'd always been and honestly, Aliana seemed like she was handling herself quite admirably.

She moved smoothly, like I remembered from our long training sessions, with the grace and beauty of a dancer, her dagger flicking out and arcing through the air before crashing into Cyron's sword. Sparks flew, and I could see the heat coming from the runes on the blade.

"It's just like you fucking elves to ruin plans that I'd laid down for decades," Cyron was saying. He was a formidable fighter himself, although his style represented a lot more brute strength than speed and dexterity. "Then again, all this is to get rid of you anyway, so it's rather fitting that there's someone of your pathetic race here to represent the rest."

Aliana didn't respond, showing no sign that the man's words were affecting her at all. She ducked and leaned backward, avoiding a slash and thrust from the man's blade in quick succession then stayed low as she pirouetted lightly, her dagger flicking out toward Cyron's neck. He avoided the strike by leaning to the side, but I could see the gleam of blood rushing from his cheek from where her dagger had struck him.

"Fuck!" Cyron cursed, touching his cheek. He took a few steps away from Aliana, speaking a few words in a language I didn't understand. The golem understood, though, as it looked away from the flashes of lightning coming from Norel's hands and turned away, ignoring the damage she was doing to its back and charging toward Aliana.

"Oh, fuck me." I had to do something.

Norel looked like she'd been injured in her fight, struggling to keep up with the monster as it picked up speed, and Aliana wouldn't stand much of a chance against Cyron *and* the golem. I had to do something.

Like what, genius?

Something stupid. Something that would hope-fully save all our lives, at the risk of mine. I was willing to take that chance.

Cyron was focused on Aliana as she picked up her pace, trying to finish him off before the golem got to her. I rushed forward, wondering why the ever-loving hell I was doing this. Cyron didn't see me until I was already on top of him. He tried to raise a barrier to stop me, but too late. I crashed into his side, knocking him to the ground with a thud.

The sword in his hands came free, clattering to the ground.

"What the...?" Cyron said as I jumped away from him, avoiding the offensive spell he cast at me with a dodge and a roll as I picked up the sword.

A golem couldn't be harder to take down than Aliana, right? True, I'd never managed that either, but there was a first time for everything, I mused. I gripped the longsword with both hands, watching the runes on the blade light up. The heat from them was scorching enough to warp the air around it. Enchanted blades were also banned by the Emperor's decree. Were there any magical laws that Cyron hadn't broken so far?

My eyes widened as I watched the golem's massive, club-like arms swinging toward me. It was slow-moving, but terrifyingly large. I felt the ground shake when they crashed into the ground behind me, narrowly missing the opportunity to turn me into paste. I gripped the sword tighter, diving between the creature's legs, following the moves Aliana had taught me during our time in the forest. It wasn't perfectly executed, but I managed to come up to one knee behind the golem before it could turn around, the glowing blade slashing at its planted leg.

It had been twisting around, trying to track me down for another try at crushing me. Now minus a leg, the movement was cut short. The half leg swung around and caught me firmly in the chest, sending me flying a good ten feet across the room to land heavily on the ground. I managed to keep my grip on the sword the whole way, even as I struggled to breathe for a few moments.

I pushed myself up, watching the golem trying and failing to keep its balance. It fell over Cyron, who was still distracted by keeping Aliana at bay with quickly-cast combat spells now that his sword was gone. He turned just in time to scream as the fifteen-foot-tall monster of rock and clay crashed on top of him. From where I was it was difficult to see, but I thought there was a small pouch in the massive creature's hand.

I groaned, clutching my side with one hand and gripping the sword with the other as I moved over to where Norel had dropped to her knees. She was trying to heal herself, but she was distracted by what was happening across the room.

"Get out of here," I said. "You're wounded. Aliana and I can handle it from here."

"I need to know she's all right," Norel whispered, trying and failing to climb to her feet. I caught her just in time to keep her from sprawling onto her face.

"Go," I said in a softer tone. "I'll make sure she's all right."

Norel nodded, taking a deep breath as I let her go. A few seconds later, she disappeared into a portal. I turned my attention back to Aliana, the golem, and Cyron.

Aliana had moved over to where the golem had fallen, tugging the pouch from the thick clay fingers. I could see Cyron still trying to get himself out from under the weight of it. *It was surprising the man had managed to survive,* I mused, clutching my side as I ran over, realizing that the creature was starting to move again. Even without a leg, it was considerably more powerful than I had thought. I was starting to regret having sent Norel on her way.

"Watch out!" I called to Aliana, who looked up and jumped away just in time to avoid being crunched by the creature's other hand. The golem started to push itself off the ground, freeing Cyron.

Aliana had put some space between her and the golem, and now closed her eyes. I could see runes rising from her arms and shoulders. Spell-casting was more powerful than combat magic, I remembered Vis telling me, but took more time to summon. I didn't know what she was trying to do, but considering the amount of power that would be required to bring the massive thing down, I didn't think she had enough time to do it.

I reached into myself, grasping at the slippery power source inside me and using the raw power from the sword in my hands. I wouldn't be able to get between the golem and Aliana in time. I needed to do something.

I closed my eyes, feeling my consciousness slip out from inside my body. I reached out, using the movement of my body to imitate my power reaching out to grab the golem by the neck. I could feel some resistance to that, but as difficult as it was for me to grasp and use my power, it was much more difficult for anything else to touch it. The 'fingers' wrapped around the golem's neck and as I gritted my teeth, trying to keep hold of it, I pulled.

The moment after I tugged, I lost my grasp on the power. It took the shuddering impact of the creature to the ground to tell me that, against all odds, what I'd tried to do had worked.

I wasn't sure how but at this point, it would be like inspecting the teeth on a gift horse.

I opened my eyes again, seeing Cyron staring at me with a gaping mouth. I remembered the conversation Vis had with Pollock about my power, and in that moment, I realized that whatever Vis had done to my parents had been on Cyron's orders. He knew about me and my power, and was surprised to see me using it.

In the moment of distraction between Cyron and

the golem, Aliana was able to complete her spell. She'd been speaking in a language I couldn't understand. As I turned to her, I could see the runes on her skin glowing blue instead of red. Her eyes were a similar color. When she extended her hand, the room was filled with the thunderous sound of a stone being split in half. First it was just a crack, but it started to grow. A massive hole appeared in the middle of the room, spreading quickly toward where the golem was starting to regain its feet. It had no sense of self-preservation, I realized, still trying to stand up and reach Aliana as it started to drop into the gaping hole opening behind it.

The hole started spreading, like Aliana didn't have much in the way of control over it. I started inching back, seeing it starting to head in my direction. I looked over at Cyron, whose legs were still broken from when the golem landed on him, desperately trying to heal himself while dragging himself away from the growing gap in the floor. He wasn't going to make it, I realized, tucking his sword into my belt and rushing over to where the floor was starting to swallow him too.

Just as he was starting to drop into the chasm, I reached out, grabbing his hand by the wrist. I had no good intentions for the man, but I didn't want him to die just yet.

He looked up at me as I helped him back to the

edge, giving him just enough purchase to keep from dropping, but not enough to be able to pull himself up.

"What are you doing?" he screamed, looking down at the growing hole in terror.

"Tell me what happened to my parents!" I demanded, feeling the anger I'd had burning inside me ever since I learned that Vis had killed them rushing up to the surface.

"Please, you have to—" Cyron pleaded but I cut him off.

"I don't have to do anything." I gripped him by the wrist, reminding him that I could just as easily pull him up as push him down. "Tell me what happened to them, and I'll consider saving your life."

"We don't have the time!" Cyron screamed, shaking his head. "Promise you won't kill me and that you'll let me go, and I'll tell you anything you want to know!"

"You won't go free, even if I save you," I snarled. "You'll be held to trial by the Emperor for your crimes. But you'll be alive if you just fucking tell me!"

In my rage, I almost missed the man's hand moving forward, arcing energy flowing through his fingers. I didn't have time to react even then, just raise my right hand in an instinctive movement to stop him. He knew he was going to die, I realized from the crazed look on his face. He was just going to take me with him.

I watched the energy he'd gathered lash out at me, striking my outstretched hand first. I felt it burn, just as hot as when I'd touched the hound's skin. To both our surprise, the power jumped back from it, hammering into Cyron's chest.

For a moment, there was a look of shock on his face as he lost his grip on the edge of the hole and realized he was falling.

"No!" I screamed. He hadn't told me. I needed to know, and maybe the only person left alive who could tell me was dropping into the darkness of what looked like a bottomless pit. I tried to reach inside myself looking for the power I was supposed to have, but it pulled away, slipping away from my grasp just like Cyron.

He disappeared into the blackness.

I pulled myself away from the edge of the hole using as much willpower as I could manage. For the craziest second, I had been tempted to dive in after him. Of all the idiotic decisions I'd made so far, that would have been my crowning achievement.

I looked down at my hand, surprised to see the runes that had been welted but partially healed were glowing again. Painfully so, but still glowing like the runes on Aliana's arms, or Cyron's for that matter. As

I thought about it, I realized that I didn't even know how they'd gotten those.

I covered my hand, wincing from the pain as Aliana moved over to me.

"Where's Cyron?" she asked, looking around.

"I tried to save him." I pushed myself to my feet. "Didn't go as well as I hoped."

Aliana looked down into the hole. She looked as disappointed as I was, but I doubted that any tears would be shed at the man's passing.

"Come on," she said, taking my hand. In an instant, we were tugged and twisted into one of her portals.

❧ 18 ❧

We arrived back at our cave, both of us stumbling forward a few steps before dropping to the ground next to each other. For the longest of moments, it was all we could do to just stare up at the roof of the cave. A moment was needed to process everything. As we lay there in silence, my mind went back to me holding Cyron's life in the balance to get him to tell me what had happened to my parents. I had been angry, in that moment, and while I did feel that my actions had been at least somewhat justified, there was a nagging feeling telling me that I had taken it just a step too far.

"I tried to get Cyron to tell me what happened to my parents," I said, finally breaking the silence between us. "I made sure he didn't fall, but then kept from pulling him up until he told me what I wanted to know."

"And you let him fall when he refused?" Aliana asked, turning over to look at me.

"The thought occurred to me," I admitted. "But no. I told him that even if he lived, he wouldn't see the outside of a cell for the rest of his days. He tried to attack me and... somehow, the spell rebounded on him and knocked him down."

"Rebounded?" Aliana asked.

"You know. Bounced off, went back to him."

"I know what rebounded means," Aliana said, grinning. "But how?"

"I don't know," I said, showing her my hand, where the runes were still branded on. "But I think this might have something to do with it."

Aliana leaned in closer, tilting her head. "I don't know what those runes are, actually."

"Anyways, they were glowing and burning afterward," I explained. "So, I think they might have had something to do with it. I'm not sure how. I didn't even intend to do anything. It just happened."

"That's how magic is supposed to be, sometimes," Aliana said with a grin, propping herself up on her elbow and leaning closer to me. "You just need to follow your basest instincts."

She leaned in and tenderly pressed her lips to mine. I reached over, threading my fingers through her silky-smooth hair and pulling her closer as her tongue slipped into my mouth, exploring and tasting me. She appeared to like what she was tasting since I felt as much as heard a long, low, delicious moan pass from her mouth to mine.

As she pulled away, my eyes stayed closed. I leaned in closer to her, wanting more. My eyes opened when she pressed a finger to my lips.

"We have one more jump to make," Aliana explained with a smile. She gripped my hand, and suddenly we were twisting through the void once more. I hadn't been expecting it so the twisting and pulling knocked the breath out of me, leaving me gasping and coughing as we came out the other end.

"I hate portals," I snarled, shaking my head and pushing myself to my feet.

Aliana didn't reply. She just shook her head and chucked.

"Where are we?" I asked, looking around.

"Welcome to my home," I heard a voice say from behind us. I whipped around, reaching for the sword that was still hanging from my belt. I wasn't sure why. We hadn't known each other for very long, but I did recognize Norel's voice.

"Your home?" I asked, looking around. "It looks surprisingly untouched by the destructive capabilities of an obsidian hellhound."

Norel looked around, a smile on her lips. "Well,

that was one of them, yes. You didn't think I had just one, did you?"

"Well, forgive a man who has none for making wrong assumptions," I replied with a grin.

"All right, all right," Aliana said, stepping in.

"I assume the two of you are here because Cyron won't be joining us?" Norel asked.

"Yes," I replied.

"Excellent," she said, indicating for us to join her. "We can sit and you two can tell me about everything I missed over a meal. I think we all need it."

On that we could agree, I realized, smiling as we moved into a room where a small feast had been prepared. There were a handful of servants waiting for us to take our seats before filling some goblets with what looked like mead. I had seen it being served, but never tasted the stuff myself.

Aliana and Norel talked, going over everything that had happened. I was probably not the best witness since I didn't understand much about what was happening, so I focused my attention on tasting the roast pheasant and ham that had been served for us. It felt like years since I'd had a proper meal like this. Well, in all honesty, I'd never really had a meal quite like this. Never this good. The bread was still warm from the oven, and combined with the soft cheese and freshly-made butter, kept me busy for most of the conversation.

"I have to say, I wouldn't have thought you had it in you, Grant," I heard Norel say. I looked up from my plate, still chewing on a pheasant drumstick as I realized I'd lost track of the conversation.

"Sorry," I mumbled through a half-full mouth. "Just hungry, is all."

"Well, yes, there is that," Norel said. "But what I meant is holding off on saving someone until he tells you what you want to know. Sure, Cyron is a stone-cold bastard, but even then, it takes a hefty pair to do something like that."

"Pair of what?" I asked, managing to swallow the rest of my food.

"I'll show you later," Aliana leaned closer and whispered in my ear.

"Wait, hold up," I said. "Cyron is a stone-cold bastard? Is? Not was?"

"Well, there is always the possibility he died," Norel said, toying with her goblet between her fingers. "But I know the man doesn't die easily. I'd say it would take more than a single fall to kill him."

Well, that was a terrifying prospect, I thought, taking a sip from the mead and wincing. It was strong enough that I could feel a burn rushing down my throat, but it was still sickeningly sweet, masking the taste of the alcohol rather masterfully. I wasn't sure if I liked it or not, yet, but considering it was all that was being served here, I had to assume it was a favorite of Norel's.

"What was Cyron looking for in that chamber, anyway?" Norel asked, looking over at Aliana.

"Oh, right!" Aliana exclaimed, pulling the pouch that I remembered seeing in the golem's hand out of nowhere in particular. "I almost forgot."

She handed it to Norel, who leaned closer to grab it from her fingers. Norel took a moment to inspect the pouch, making sure there weren't any wards of protection on it that might prove dangerous. Once satisfied, she pulled it open. Her eyes widened and she gasped, dropping it onto the table like it had burned her fingers.

"What is it?" I asked, but Aliana didn't seem to hear me as she leaned in to see what it was. A pair of golden orbs, each as large as my fist, rolled over the table toward us. They were translucent, both of them an interesting combination of red and gold. There was something in the center but I couldn't really make out what they were.

"Are those dragon eyes?" Aliana asked, a note of horror in her voice, which cracked. I looked at her, placing a hand on her shoulder and squeezing.

"It's a good thing Cyron didn't get his hands on those," Norel said, trying to gather her composure, although she refused to look at the orbs directly. "If taking over the empire was his goal, they would have delivered it to him handily."

"What are dragon eyes?" I asked, picking one of them up. It was warm to the touch, and softer than I would have thought.

"The eyes of a dragon," Aliana said softly, her voice still breaking.

"Oh," I grunted, needing a moment to process that before realizing what I was holding. "Oh!" I dropped it onto the table. "Wait, dragons. They're myths, right? They don't really exist. Stories and fairy tales, yes?"

"They are as real as djinn are," Norel said, tossing the pouch to me. I quickly and gingerly pushed the orbs back into it and pulled the strings shut, hoping I never had to open them again. I'd need time later to process that, on top of everything else, dragons were actually real and we had a pair of their eyes on the table.

I'd suddenly lost my appetite.

❧ 19 ❧

The meal was finished so Norel guided us out of the room. Like her other house, this place was something of a maze. Thankfully, with Norel there to guide us we found our way through quickly and easily, without getting lost. I remembered what Aliana had said about Norel liking mazes and couldn't help but wonder where that particular fascination stemmed from.

Norel opened the door into a bedroom that was larger than any room I'd ever spent the night in. The bed was larger than the room I had back in Vis' manor, while the golden glow from the sun setting outside complemented the various candles inside. There was a bronze bath set up, although without water in it for the moment.

"You can rest here," Norel told me with a smile.

"After the day we've all had, I can only imagine that sleep is definitely in order. I have a room for you too, Aliana. I'll come and wake the both of you in the morning. We have a lot to discuss."

"If you don't mind, sister," Aliana said softly. "I think I'd like to stay here with Grant for the moment. We too have a great deal to talk about."

Norel paused, tilting her head as she considered us, and then chuckled.

"Very well," she said, moving back toward the door. "Enjoy your conversation."

She stepped out, closing the door behind her. I looked around the room again. I had seen buildings smaller than this, I realized, moving further in. Sure, for someone who lived in this kind of opulence all their lives this was probably no more than barely acceptable, but to me, it was a palace.

"So, what did you want to tal... oh," I said, turning around to see Aliana walking away from the closed door, her clothes already left behind as she approached me.

"Believe me when I say, Grant," she whispered as she came in closer to me, "that talking is the last thing on my mind right now."

My mouth was suddenly dry and words failed to come in response. Which was all right, I assumed, since talking was the last thing on her mind. Aliana stepped closer, pulling the ruined pieces of armor from my body and then helping me out of my clothes. Once I was as naked as she was, she pushed me onto the bed, surprising me. I sank into the luxurious softness of the massive bed, enjoying it for a moment before she moved over to join me on it. She climbed over me, straddling my hips and letting me feel every inch of her soft yet firm body gliding over me as she peppered kisses over my stomach, chest and neck, until she finally reached my lips.

"You're so fucking beautiful," I whispered as she looked down at me, her hair falling to put a curtain between us and the rest of the world. My hands moved up over her sides, slowly stroking and touching. *Not tentative, but not yet bold,* I mused, running my fingers lightly over the smooth skin of her hips, her waist, and then down to her ass. I could see her wings fluttering gently in excitement as I smacked her right cheek firmly.

"You're pretty damn delicious yourself," she murmured, leaning closer and kissing my lips softly as she pressed her firm breasts into my chest. She reached between us, gripping my quickly-hardening cock and giving it a few strokes before pushing it up between her thighs and letting it glide between her pussy's lips.

"Oh gods," I whispered, my hips thrusting upward, more out of instinct than actual intention. She pushed the thick head down to her warm entrance, letting it tease there for a moment, moaning without letting our lips part before sinking down on it slowly. I could feel her body tightening around me, making my eyes bulge as a wave of pleasure rushed through my body.

"Fuck!" I gasped once she pulled away from the kiss. I could see her eyes rolling up, her mouth dropping open as she started to ride me slowly, grinding her hips over mine, leaving me firmly buried inside her for a few long moments before rising and sinking again.

I could feel her body gliding over mine again and again, and each time was like the first, sending shots of sensation climbing up my spine. My hips started to rise to meet hers, only making the moans grow in intensity. She took hold of my hands, tangling them with hers as she rose, straightening, giving me a full view of her delicious body as she kept on riding me. I could feel her inner muscles gripping at my thick, throbbing shaft, telling me that she was close. There were other signs, too, like the sight of her body tensing over me, as her eyes closed, and her squeezing my hands more and more until her hips started bucking into me.

"Oh... Grant! Grant!" she cried, not bothering to keep it down. She slowed, her thrusts losing a bit of momentum as she kept moving her body over mine, pulling my hands up to her breasts. I needed little encouragement to pay attention to the deliciously heavy and soft orbs, squeezing and kneading them slowly before pulling away and toying with her nipples for a long moment.

Her eyes opened and she looked down at me, enjoying the sight of my naked body below hers for a moment before seeing the hunger that I was radiating. I was far from finished with her. She grinned cheekily, biting her bottom lip and tilting her head, extending an unspoken challenge.

I didn't need to be invited twice.

I picked her up and tossed her onto the bed beside me, keeping her facing down as I quickly slipped behind her. My hands ran over her sides as I bit my lip. I wasn't sure how, but I could feel my cock, which was still dripping with her cum, growing even harder as I pushed myself into her from behind. She gasped and let out a long, hungry, tempting moan, pushing back into my initial thrust. I kept them coming, slowly at first, but picking up the pace with each thrust. I could feel and hear my hips slapping against her firm ass each time I bottomed out inside her. I kept pushing, grunting each time. One hand moved up to have better purchase on her shoulder, yanking her back to take me in deeper and harder each time, with her prolonged moans breaking in time with my cock filling her. Her wings were fluttering and moving disjointedly in her excitement, pressing into my extended arm.

"Ali," I whispered, my eyes closing as I felt her pussy tightening around me again. Her moans turned to broken cries each time I pounded inside her. She lost the strength to keep herself on her hands and knees in front of me. I didn't mind, straddling her ass and continuing, feeling her coming again in quick succession, her wings coming up to somehow wrap around me as she did.

"Gra-a-a-a-ant!" she screamed, her hands gripping the rich silk sheets we were fucking on. The bed was rocking underneath us, its strong construction keeping it from collapsing, but still creaking and shuddering each time I hammered my cock home.

"Please fuck me, Grant," she gasped, her voice hoarse, eyes still closed. "Fuck me harder... oh... fuck... yes..." She reached around, her fingers digging into my ass, helping to push me deeper inside her as my hands settled on the bed over her shoulders.

"Cum inside me!" she gasped, losing her grip on my sweaty skin and retuning her hands to the sheets. "Please... Fill me up... Please, Grant!"

I was in such a state that my comprehension of what she was saying was limited at best, but the meaning of what she wanted plus the way she was pushing back into my thrusts were not lost on me. I could feel myself just on the edge of bliss, my body tensing, feeling her pussy wrapping around me, gripping my cock tighter, making it impossible not to buck my hips down into her, filling her up over and over again.

The pleasure lasted longer than I thought possible, but as I finally dropped onto the bed beside her, gasping for breath, I realized it hadn't lasted long enough. *I wanted more,* I thought, looking out the window into the setting sun.

She needed just as much time to recover as I, slowly pushing herself up from the bed, her arms still trembling as she moved over to lay her head on my chest, one wing joining her arm in draping across me.

"Fuck, Grant," she whispered, eyes drifting shut. "Remind me again, why we haven't been doing that all this time?"

"I have no idea," I said, tilting my head down to press a kiss on top of her head, between her horns.

❧ 20 ❧

"S o," I asked, leaning into the seat provided for me. "Do you actually like mead?"

Norel tilted her head, smiling as she looked at her goblet. "I do. It's one of my favorite drinks, though I'll admit it's something of an acquired taste. I have an insatiable sweet tooth, so it appeals to my need for sweetness as well as my need for alcohol."

I nodded. "I'll admit that my knowledge of drinks is limited, but I don't think I could ever get used to this. It has a cloying taste, and the more of it I drink, the worse it gets."

Norel grinned and nodded. "Noted. I'll be sure to procure something more to your tastes for next time."

"Appreciated," I said, raising my goblet and making a sour face in quick succession, realizing it meant that I would have to drink another sip of the stuff I'd just been complaining about. I did so, wincing as the sweet liquid went down my gullet.

"To business," Norel said softly, placing her goblet on a small table next to her seat and picking up a couple papers from it. Aliana took a deep breath, leaning her head on my shoulder with a smile.

"The search for Braire has been somewhat unsuccessful," Norel said, scowling at the first paper, quickly throwing it aside like it had just offended her.

"Braire?" I asked, looking at Aliana.

"Did you forget that there was a third sister?" she asked, looking up into my eyes. She kissed my neck before settling back onto my shoulder.

"Oh... right," I said. I had forgotten, but I wasn't going to admit that even under torture.

"The better news is that those nobles who are still loyal to the emperor have had a good deal to say about Cyron's recent actions," Norel continued. "I've handpicked a few that I've seen to be honest and loyal—as much as you can expect from these nobles, anyway—and I want you two to meet with them."

"I'm more than willing to bring in allies for our fight," Aliana said, her voice serious even though she remained snuggled close to me. "But I don't think it's time to share the fact that we have a couple of dragon eyes. As far as I'm concerned, nobody except those present need to know we have an artifact with that much power in our possession."

"Agreed," Norel said with a firm nod.

"Agreed," I said, not really sure why I was agreeing, but the two of them seemed to know what they were talking about.

"Those still loyal were very interested by the presence of a rogue mage among us," Norel continued. "They would like to meet with you in person, Grant, before granting you the rank of Varion, a mage's position with the Lancers. It meant shield, or defender, in Elvish. Considering all that you've done to keep the empire from falling to ruin, I don't think there's much you could do to prevent them from granting it to you anyway. That said, I have every confidence in your creativity, so it would be best if we brush up on your court protocol first, wouldn't you say?"

I nodded, realizing that Aliana's hands had drifted down to my pants. Norel saw this too, raising a judgmental eyebrow as she watched Aliana idly stroke me.

Norel smirked while picking up a cluster of pale white grapes from a plate on the table, putting the rest of the papers aside for later.

"Do you wish me to give you two some privacy, sister?" she asked, plucking the grapes from the cluster and popping them into her mouth one by one.

"No," Aliana whispered, slipping out of her seat to

take a position between my knees, which she spread to accommodate herself. "Stay. Watch."

I raised my eyebrows in surprise, my mouth opening to voice a protest. It was cut short somewhere in my throat when Aliana dipped her head to press a light kiss to my cock through my trousers. A soft yet visible shudder drifted up my body as she took hold of the waistband of my pants and pulled them down low enough to let my quickly-hardening shaft jump free from its confines. I looked up for a moment to see Norel settling back into her seat, watching us thoughtfully as she slowly ate the grapes.

I turned my head back as Aliana cradled my balls in her warm hand, running her wet, agile tongue up the underside of my cock from the sack all the way to its thick and throbbing head, circling around it a few times before taking it into her mouth.

I groaned softly, my hand coming down to settle on her head, fingers toying at the roots of her horns as her head started bobbing on my cock, filling her mouth with it over and over again, sucking it in and keeping it up as she pulled away, drawing a soft gasp from me.

I could see Norel shifting in her seat. The way she was biting her bottom lip told me that she was enjoying the show, but I couldn't bring myself to look up at her. Ever since that first time, it had been difficult to keep my hands off of Aliana, and from the way she was acting she felt the same, although she was unhindered by whatever drawbacks I was feeling.

As a shudder of pleasure rushed through my body, raising goosebumps all the way, I wasn't entirely sure what those drawbacks were. I would remember presently. Maybe when she wasn't polishing my cock with her mouth.

Maybe.

While keeping one hand on my balls, she let the other grip the base of my cock, stroking it quickly as her head moved in time, her eyes turning up to look at me as my eyes rolled back in my head, another jolt of pleasure making me unintentionally thrust myself deeper into her mouth. She grinned and moaned, vibrating her voice around the sensitive head, inching me closer and closer to orgasm.

I looked again, seeing Norel looking me firmly in the eyes as I felt my cock twitching inside Aliana's mouth, filling it with my warm seed. I wasn't sure how or why but having her around to watch us just made it all that much more enjoyable. I had always thought that sex was supposed to be something between two people, but the way she was watching as I came in her sister's mouth was shattering those expectations. I found my mind wandering to thoughts of having both Norel and Aliana on their knees in front of me.

Aliana pulled away, staying on her knees as she

smacked and licked her lips, letting her tongue back out to clean my cock thoroughly.

Norel got to her feet. I thought I caught the gentlest of wobbles in her knees as she did, but it disappeared quickly. She picked up her goblet and quickly drained it to the last drop in a single gulp.

"Well, as enjoyable as that was," Norel said, "I'm afraid I still have business to attend to today." She moved away, and I couldn't help but watch as her hips swayed seductively in parting.

"Don't worry," Aliana said, drawing my attention back down to her as she grinned coyly. "We'll get her involved soon enough."

"What?" I asked, my voice thick and throatier than I thought it would be. I thought about denying that interest for a moment, but I didn't think I could have made my thoughts any more obvious.

"I know that woman better than I know myself," Aliana said with a grin. "I wasn't even looking at her, and I could tell that it was all she could do not to hop on your cock herself."

"I think you know that you're more than enough woman for me, Ali," I said with a grin, playing with her hair.

"Oh, come now," Aliana said, leaning in to press a kiss to my cock, which was still hard despite having cum a few minutes earlier. "Are you telling me you can't imagine having two tongues doing this?" She flicked hers over the head slowly, sending a long rush of arousal coursing through my body again.

I shuddered, reaching into myself and taking firm grasp of the power in me. I could feel the runes branded in my hand starting to glow, with only a tickle of a burning sensation as I ran the same hand through her hair. It took a few seconds to have effect. I'd been practicing a bit, but this was the first time I was testing it on her.

The shuddered gasp coming from her as she lost her balance, needing to grasp me to keep from falling, over told me that my practice had not gone to waste. She turned her eyes up to me, hooded with lust as she licked her lips.

"Oh... You bastard." She moaned, her lips close enough to my cock that I could feel them moving.

"You have no idea," I growled, keeping the connection that was flooding her pussy with pleasure alive as I gripped the back of her head firmly. "Now, let's try that again. Just the one tongue for now."

She nodded, even as I could feel her body tightening, right on the edge of an orgasm as I filled her mouth with my cock. I wasn't far behind, and when I reached orgasm again, everything was perfect.

"I'm coming for you," a distant voice said.

My eyes blinked, my heart racing. A glance around showed it hadn't been Aliana, as she was still lying there, smiling with her eyes closed. No, it wasn't her voice, anyway. It wasn't Norel's, either.

When I opened my mind to listen more, it didn't return. But I had no doubt it was there, some dark force judging by the tingling fear it left crawling up my spine.

I stood, grabbing my clothes. "My magic... it's not enough."

Aliana opened her eyes, frowned. "It did the job."

"For what's ahead, I mean."

"Ah." She pushed herself up. Pouted. "As much as I'd love nothing more than to lie here in your embrace, you have a point. We have a lot of training to do, if you're truly going to be this Varion of ours."

My eyes roamed over her perfect body, loving what we had. What, apparently, I'd soon have with Norel as well. And maybe the third sister? Damn, I was getting greedy.

Regardless, all of that could be much better appreciated when the fighting was over, when the evil was defeated... whatever form it took. And when that voice, whoever it belonged to, would never bother me again.

ABOUT THE AUTHOR

Mark Albany is fan of epic fantasy and living life to its fullest. He hopes to embrace such story telling as Game of Thrones and Venom in this tale, and add one more spot of fun in your life.

For fans of Mark Lawrence, Will Wight, David Estes, and Brandon Sanderson.

Check out my Facebook Group if you'd like to chat more!

https://www.facebook.com/groups/2474767712539848/

And I started a newsletter: https://www.subscribepage.com/MarkAlbany